## Acknowledgments

To my friends, family and readers of *The Loft*, *Catherine's Choice* and *Sarah* who encouraged me to continue writing. To my husband, without whom, *The Journals* would not have been written.

Cover design by

Michael A. Swanson

# The Journals

by

## K.M. SWAN

# ~1~

She glanced at her watch as she turned right onto the ramp and exited the freeway. She would be there in twenty minutes, well, thirty minutes really. She would stop at the store to pick up a few groceries. Four hours earlier she had called her boss and told him of her plans.

Standing in her nightgown, she hurriedly dialed the number and waited for the secretary with the saccharin voice to answer.

"Carson Realty. How may I help you?"

"Lillie, it's Karin. Is Brad in?" Brad Carson was the owner and was always there early in the morning.

"Yes, but he's on another line. Do you want to wait? Oh just a sec, I think he's hung up. I'll put you through."

"Thanks."

"Brad Carson here."

"Brad, it's Karin. I won't be in today," she said, hesitantly.

"What do you mean? It's Friday, remember? You're showing the Garret house at nine-thirty."

"Well, I can't. I'm taking a sick day today and then a week of vacation. I'll be back a week from Monday. Is that okay with you?"

"Is something wrong, Karin? It better be important. We've got a lot of houses right now," he told her.

"My grandmother has left me her lake house. Remember she died a few weeks ago?"

"Of course I remember."

"Well, I have to go there and take care of things. You know," she added.

It was a bit of a lie. She didn't really need to go to the lake now to take care of Grandma's things; she needed to go now to get *away*.

"I'm sure Corrine will show the house today, if you ask her, and she'll be able to take some of my work next week, too, I think. She doesn't have very much right now," she told him.

"Yeah, I guess she could. Sure you're alright, Karin?" he asked.

"I'm fine. It's just something that I have to do. Thanks a bunch, boss man. I'll work extra hard when I get back."

"You always do; that's why we'll miss you. Take care now." He was a great boss and truly a gentleman. She had been lucky to find that job.

She drove into the small parking lot in front of the equally small store and got out of the car, not bothering to lock it. There was no need to here. She stretched her legs some. She had been driving for three and a half hours, and she wasn't used to sitting that long. It was eleven-thirty in the morning, and the sun was shining brightly. It was a beautiful day.

Entering the store, she pushed her sun glasses up onto her forehead. It was dark and cool in there, compared to outside. She recognized no one in the store today, remembering a time when she had known everyone. Picking up a small basket, she began to fill it with a few necessities: bread, jam, eggs and a quart of milk. She would come back in the morning and do some real shopping. As she headed for the checkout, she grabbed a chilled bottle of wine from the cooler.

"Are you new to these parts?" the checker asked, chewing gum while she talked.

"Not really, but I haven't been here for a while. I came here every summer as a girl, though," she offered. The girl looked at her questioningly, as if she wanted further explanation. She didn't get any. Karin paid for her purchases and smiled her thanks.

Back in the car she felt safe again, safe from people and their unending chatter. In ten minutes she was parked in front of the house. She smiled, remembering how they had argued about that.

Grandpa always said, "The lake is the front; any darn fool knows that." But she and Grandma thought that the road was the front.

She unlocked the door and stepped inside, shutting it behind her. Leaning against it, she closed her eyes and thought that it was wonderful to be alone, finally. She had nine whole days to figure out what was really going on in her life. She hoped it would be enough time.

She walked around the place, giving it a quick once over. Everything seemed to be in order. She put the food away, then took a glass from the cupboard, found an old cork screw in one of the drawers, picked up the cold wine and went out the door to the lake. It was hot and humid, but a cool breeze off the water took care of that. She walked down the wooden stairs that led to the pier, carefully watching for toads and garter snakes. The lake was calm and soothing. She sat on the bench that her grandfather had bolted to the pier all those years ago, remembering how he had dropped one of bolts in the water, and fussed and cussed, until he finally took off his shoes and waded into the lake to try to find it.

She poured a glass of the chardonny and took a sip. There were five sailboats on the lake that she could see. "This is so peaceful," she whispered, unable to recall feeling this calm in some time. She stayed that way for quite awhile, just watching the lake, wondering if water had the same effect on other people as it did on her. It was tranquilizing. She wasn't sure if it was because we came from the water all those millions of years ago, crawling from the sea on our bellies and evolving into what we are today, or if was our remembrance of the womb and how safe we were then.

Kicking off her sandals she got off the bench and sat on the edge of the pier, her bare feet dangling in the water; it was cool. She splashed her feet, and suddenly she was Karina again; she was ten years old.

"My name is Ka-ree-na," she told everyone she met. People tended to put an "a" on the end of Karin, which is how one would think it would be pronounced.

"It's Ka-ree-na," she said over and over until at the age of eighteen she simply dropped the "a", much to her mother's chagrin. Her mother had made up both her daughters' names and was very proud of her so called creativity. Her sister was Karola and had dropped her "a", as well. Karin thought that if she had a dollar for every time she had pronounced her name for someone, she could surely quit her job.

Her stomach growled, bringing her back to the present. She looked at her watch. She had been sitting there for over an hour. She pulled her feet out of the water and let them dry in the sun. Slipping her feet into her sandals, she picked up the wine bottle and glass and headed up to the house. When she got to the top of the hill, she stopped to look at the house. It was very different from when she and her mother had first come here to spend the summer with her grandparents. It was a year-around-home now, but then it had been a summer cottage.

The first summer they had to use the outhouse. She doubted her daughter would even know what that was, but that was thirty years ago. By the second year Grandpa had put in a toilet, sink, walk-in shower and enclosed it with walls. Everyone was much happier that summer.

Karin thought it odd that she and her mother always came, but never her dad or her sister. Her dad had to work, but she thought her sister had missed out on a lot by staying home. Karol was four years older than Karin and loved the freedom she had alone all day while her dad worked. Karin wondered how her mother could have left her sister

there all summer, and thought maybe she had done
the same thing. Her daughter was alone all day while
her husband worked. "It's not the same," she told
herself, feeling she was better than her mother had
been.

"It's only for nine days," she muttered, as she
went into the house. She called home to let them
know she arrived safely. The answering machine
picked up and she listened to her own voice saying
that they couldn't come to phone just now, but to
please leave a message.

"Hi, it's me," she said to the machine. "I got here
about an hour ago and everything is fine. I'll talk
to you soon; call if you want. I love you both. Bye."
With that done, she wondered where her daughter
was, but forced the thought from her mind.

"You're here to escape all that," she scolded herself. "So don't waste time worrying." She couldn't
help but worry, though. Kaitlin had changed so
much in the past year. She was twelve years old
now, still a little girl in many ways, but that would
change soon, and it was a rough world out there.
Sometimes she wished she could keep her this young
forever.

Kaitlin had been begging to baby-sit the kids down
the street. Karin thought it was too much respon-
sibility for someone so young, but her husband dis-
agreed. She was a very trustworthy child, and after
all, it's close to home, he had argued. She did sit
for Cindy and Don's kids often, but that was next
door. Karin didn't know the people down the street
very well and they wanted someone to watch the
kids a few days a week all summer. She would just

have to think about that another time.

After some eggs with toast and jam, Karin began to clean the place a bit. It wasn't really dirty but needed a light going over, as her grandma used to say. She would sleep in Grandma's bed while she was here, not in the spare room where she and her mother had always slept. She missed her grandmother and wanted to be in her room with her things. She took the sheets off the bed, put them in the washing machine and began to tidy up the room. Some prescription bottles were still on the dresser next to her grandmother's lotion and cold cream. She threw out the pills and put some lotion on her hands. It smelled like Grandma, and she started to cry. Sitting on the bed, she blew her nose and looked at the picture on the nightstand. It was a photograph, taken many years before, of her grandparents, standing down on the pier. They were both smiling and Grandpa was holding Grandma close to his side. It was another time. She would keep this picture for herself.

With Grandma's lavender sheets hanging out on a makeshift clothes line, Karin began to look through the cupboards. She found some chicken noodle soup and an unopened box of saltine crackers; that would be her dinner. She started making a list of things she would need for the week ahead.

After a supper of soup, Karin poured a glass of wine and gingerly made her way down to the lake. The sun was setting behind her, but she wanted one more look at the lake before going to bed. She would get up before the sun tomorrow, so she could watch it rise over the lake. It was a spectacular sight, and she never tired of watching it. As a girl, she and Grandma would often get up early to see it. It looked to her, then, like millions of diamonds dancing on top of the lake, sparkling for all to see.

She finished her wine and walked slowly up the wooden stairs. She was so *tired*. She hadn't even worked today, yet she was exhausted. Back in the house she locked the doors, got ready for bed and turned out the lights. She left the window open in Grandma's bedroom and cuddled under the covers. The night air was cool and fragrant. She thought about her grandma who had lived to be ninety years old but was never the same after her daughter, Karin's mother, had died five years before.

Grandpa had died when he was eighty-five years old. Grandma was then eighty and missed him desperately, but took his death in stride. The death of her daughter was something else.

"Parents are not meant to bury their children, Karina. It's just not the way of things. It's not the proper order; it should have been me. I'm ready to go and be with your grandfather. I'm eighty-five years, old for God's sake." She had said it again and again. Karin was only thirty-five and felt that she was too young to lose her mother. She wondered if there was any real rhyme or reason to this life and drifted off to sleep. Her dreams took her back thirty years in time.

~~~

"Hey, Karina! Come down here and look what I found. Hurry!" her cousin, Sonny, shouted from somewhere down by the lake.

He and his mother, who was Karina's

8

mother's younger sister, were visiting for the weekend.

"Where are you?" she hollered, running as fast as she could down the wooden steps to the lake. He was holding up a fish net with something in it.

"What is it?" she asked. He reached into the net and pulled out a crayfish and stuck it up to her face.

"Yuck, what is it?" she asked again, wrinkling up her nose.

"I think it's a baby lobster. Yup, that's what it is," he said, with authority in his voice. He was eleven, one year older than Karina and a grade ahead in school which, in his mind, made him far superior to his female cousin.

"Yoo-hoo," Grandma called from top of the stairs.

"You kids come on up and have lunch now."

"Coming, Grandma," Karina yelled back. "What are you going to do with that lobster?" she asked Sonny.

"Don't know," he replied. "Maybe I'll cook him.

They turn red when you do, ya know."

"Throw him back in, you meany!" Karina cried.

"Why would you want to kill him? Come on, throw him back and hurry up, Grandma's waiting for us."

"Okay, I will, you sissy," he said, and

9

added, *"Girls."*

Up in the cottage, Grandma had their sandwiches on the table and was pouring milk for them.

"Where's Mom?" Karina asked.

"Yeah, where's mine?" Sonny wondered.

"The moms have gone into town to do some shopping. They'll be back for supper. Grandpa should be in then, too."

Grandpa was out fishing and had brought his lunch along. He was in his glory. He was sixty-five years old, had just retired and bought this cottage. His plan was to eventually fix it up so they could live in it all year long. They loved this part of the country and would be happy to live out their days here. It would take a lot of work, though: new roof, insulation, an addition for a furnace, washer and dryer and storage. He wanted a garage, too, but hadn't yet figured out where to put it. His first priority was an indoor toilet. This being the first year, they were forced to use the out house. At least they had running water in the kitchen. Some people still had a hand pump in the yard.

"Where are Sonny and Aunt Millie going to sleep, Grandma?" Karina asked, with her mouth full of sandwich.

"Well, Millie will sleep in your place with your mother, and you and Sonny will have to share the daybed in the big room. It opens up, so you'll have lots of room," she said. The kids thought that would be great! The adults would be in their bedrooms and the two of them would be in the big room that faced the lake. "Too bad they don't have doors on the bedrooms instead of those stupid curtains on a pole; maybe we could sneak out after they go to sleep," Sonny whispered to Karina so Grandma couldn't hear.

"Maybe we can anyway," she whispered back. "We just have to be real quiet," she added. Sonny thought she might not be so bad after all. For a girl anyway.

That night they had pretended to be sleeping and waited until the old iron beds with lumpy mattresses, that held the adults, were quiet and the soft snoring began. They quietly left the cottage.

The moon was full, so it was nearly light outside. That took away some of the need on Sonny's part to act brave. "Have you ever looked down the holes in the outhouse, Karina?"

"No! Yuck, why would I?"

"I dare you. Here take this flashlight, and shine it down there. I dare you," he challenged her.

"No, that's sickening."

"You're too chicken."

"Am not!"

"Are too!"

"Okay, give me the damn flashlight, but you stay out here."

"But you have to leave the door open, so I can see that you really do it." He was impressed; not only was she was going to do it, she had said a swear word, too. She kept her eyes shut tight, held her nose and aimed the light down the hole. "Oh, this is awful. Yuck, it's sickening! I don't believe you made me do this," she said and carried on like that for a few minutes.

"Give me that light, you sissy," he grumbled and grabbed it from her. He took a good look for himself then covered his mouth with his hand and ran out the door. He couldn't get out of there fast enough. Karina heard him gag and wondered what girls saw in boys anyway. She sure hadn't figured it out yet.

They wandered around for awhile and then went down to the lake. It looked different at night; the water was dark and scary. An owl hooted in a nearby tree, and the two of them scrambled up the wooden steps almost tripping over each other.

"What *was* that?" he asked.

"An owl, I think," she whispered. "It was so close and loud, I thought it might swoop down and peck us or something."

"Look at all the birds flying out over the lake," he said. "Wait a minute, birds go to bed when the sun goes down," he thought aloud. He remembered learning that somewhere. "What are they then?" she asked.

"Must be bats," he said, heading for the

cottage. "Shit, they *are* bats!"

"Let's go back in, Sonny. I don't like it out here at night, I guess." They opened the door quietly and crept into their bed.

# ~2~

She woke early the next morning, without the aid
of an alarm clock. That was very unusual for her,
but then life was so different here. She pulled on
her robe and went to the kitchen to start the coffee. She wondered just how old the coffee grounds
were, but they were in the fridge, so she thought
they would be okay. The place hadn't been empty
too long, really. Grandma had a stroke, went to the
hospital for a week, then to a nursing home and
died in one month. That was three weeks ago. Karin
had spent as much time with her as she possibly
could, with her job and family. The nursing home
was one hour away from where she lived. All this
had taken a toll on Karin. Her job was demanding,
her daughter was at a worrisome age, to say the
least, and her husband was distant, and then,
Grandma . . . .

As the coffee dripped, she went to the bedroom
where she put on some jeans, a sweatshirt and stuck
her bare feet into an old pair of loafers. The birds
were starting their usual chorus and the day was
about to begin. She poured a mug of coffee and

headed down to the lake. She felt alone in the world and that pleased her. No one was out early, today. She sat sideways on the bench, so she could put up her feet and wait for the sun. In minutes it started, just a slim bright curve on the horizon, steadily rising until the lake was dancing with diamonds.

Oh, she missed this part of life, watching the world wake. Everything was different here - the sounds, the smells, the sights. The birds became louder, the chipmunks were scurrying up and down the wooden steps, searching for food, and the breeze off the lake felt cool. It looked like it would be another beautiful day. She finished her coffee and went back up to the house.

The phone rang, startling her. "Who would be calling now?" she muttered. She went to the wall phone in the kitchen and lifted the receiver to her ear.

"Hello," she said.

"Karin, it's me," he said, softly.

"Oh, hi, Brian."

"Did I wake you?" he asked.

"No. I was down by the lake watching the sunrise," she answered.

"I called you last night and you weren't there," he said, questioningly.

"I was probably down by the lake; you know how I love it. Did you get my message?"

"Yes, that's why I called back. You left in such a rush. Are you okay?"

"Yes, I'm all right. You know I have to get all this stuff done here." She really wasn't sure what that meant.

"Well, do you need any help? I could come up and give you a hand," he said, tentatively.

"Oh, no. Don't do that. I'm fine. I really need some time alone, I think, Brian. I feel like I'm coming apart. Is Kaitlin all right?" she asked, hoping to change the subject.

"Sure, she's fine. She might start babysitting the neighbor's kids down the street. I told her it would be okay if she wanted to. It would be a little money for her. What do you think?"

"Oh, that's fine." She didn't want to think about that now. She just didn't.

"Well, I miss you, Honey. Are you staying all week?" He wished she wouldn't.

"Yes, I think it will take that long to settle everything here," she said, then cleared her throat to make it sound important. "I'll be home on Sunday, back to work on Monday of course."

"Of course," he said. "I love you."

"Me, too," she said. "Bye."

Shopping took up most of that first morning. She would go into town today and avoid the curious, gum-chewing checker at the neighborhood grocery. The supermarket was only a mile or so farther and had more to choose from. She would stock up for the rest of her stay, so she wouldn't need to return. The little store was handy for milk and things like that, but the supermarket was better for big shopping.

When she arrived back at the house from her shopping trip, she noticed a very old man walking around the yard. It looked like . . . "it couldn't be. Could it?" she asked herself.

"Pete? Is that you?" she asked.

"Karina? Little Karina," the old man replied. "Yes it's me. I thought I saw lights on in the house last night, just wondered who was here."

"How have you been, Pete? It's so good to see you!" She couldn't believe he was still alive. They had all called him "old Pete" nearly thirty years ago.

"Not too bad. I have some arthritis in my knees, and I don't hear too good, but I can't complain."

"Where are you living now, Pete?" she asked, remembering the shack he had lived in back then. It had been three lots north of their cottage.

"Well, over yonder, where I always lived. We tore down the old place and built a small house," he said, rubbing his chin as he thought about it. "I think it's been eighteen or twenty years ago now. I miss your grandmother. She was a good woman. We helped each other out towards the end."

Karin wondered how old he was and tried to think of a polite way to find out. "That's nice of you. I miss her, too. I wish I had come up here every summer like I did when I was a kid. But you know how that goes. You get married, have a family and you get consumed," she told him.

"How old a woman was she? If you don't mind my asking?"

"She was ninety, but you would never have known it until the end."

"That's sure the truth. I didn't know she was older than me." He grinned and told her that he was eighty-six. He was fifty-six years old when they all had called him old Pete. Hard to believe. Fifty-six didn't seem old to her now. He had a weathered look, as though he had worked outside all his life, and it made him appear older. They had known him for years, but no one knew him well. He was very private, and she was a little surprised that he had gotten close to Grandma.

He took off his hat and scratched his head. She noticed that his hair was all white now. "So how long will you be staying?" he asked.

"I'll be here for a week or so. I have to be back at work one week from Monday," she said, eager now to get inside to put away her groceries.

"Well, if you need anything, I'll be around. I can still do a little something."

"Thank you, Pete. And thank you for helping Grandma."

"Ah, shucks. She did more for me when I think about it. She always had a little leftover food that she couldn't possibly eat, she would tell me, and something fresh baked. 'You'll be doing me a favor if you take it, Pete,' she would say. Yeah, I miss her. Well, I'll let you get back to your business. I'll be talkin' to you," he said, tipping his hat and walking down the blacktop road to his home, whistling as he went. She carried in the grocery bags and smiled as she thought about how long she had known Pete. She couldn't remember if he had a wife or not. She only remembered him, always alone.

~~~

She was starting to unwind and feel contented. She really needed this. The weather was perfect again today, with blue skies and white fluffy clouds, but it didn't matter. The rain never bothered them

18

here. They would simply sit on the big porch in the old chairs and wait it out, unless it stormed; that was a different story. Then everyone ran to grab swim suits and towels off the clothes line, close car windows, get the cottage closed and if Grandpa was out on the lake, pray he would make it home in time. She smiled as she fixed her lunch. She remembered everything so vividly now that she was back here; it seemed like yesterday.

All the windows were open in the big room that faced the lake and the curtains were blowing softly. This was the room where they had all gathered. There were lots of windows on either side of the door and the view of the lake was breathtaking. They had left this room pretty much the same when the cottage was renovated as everyone loved it so. Of course it was now carpeted and the walls and ceiling were finished, but the space and the view remained.

She remembered when the walls were painted plywood and the floor was an awful green colored linoleum. The table was large and none of the chairs had matched. The daybed, an old couch, a few chairs, odd tables and lamps didn't begin to fill the room. So when the bathroom was added, Grandpa put it at the south end of this large space and it remained " the big room." The kitchen, which was small and at the north end of the cottage, was fully equipped, but not large enough to eat in. It could be entered from either of the living rooms. Most meals were eaten in the big room, because of the lake view.

From the big room, french doors with small panes

of glass led to the road side of the cottage and the other, smaller, living room. A large table was in the middle of that room with more miss-matched straight back chairs. The door leading out was in the center of the wall, with windows on either side. This room was always dark and cool, even when the sun was setting because of two enormous pine trees in the yard.

In one corner of this room stood a wood-burning stove for chilly nights and in another, an old china cabinet that was filled with a hodgepodge of things: chipped antique cups and saucers, knick-knacks, carnival glasses and just plain junk. On either side of this room were the bedrooms, which had housed old iron beds and dressers with mirrors that had lost some reflectiveness long before. The lights in these bedrooms were in the ceiling and turned on and off with a pull string that Grandma attached a stack of old buttons to, making them easier to find in the dark. She remembered all of this now. They'd had such fun then . . . .

~~~

"Why is Elvira coming over tonight for cards?" Grandpa asked.

"How many times do I have to tell you, Carl? She's coming tonight because Millie and Sonny will be here this weekend. She doesn't want to intrude on us Saturday night."

"Sorry, Lizzie Beth. I forgot." Grandma smiled and shook her head. He always called her that to tease her. Everyone else called her Beth, short for Elizabeth, but not Carl. Karina loved to listen to her grandparents banter back and forth. She wished her parents talked more to each other. She wondered, too, why her mother didn't seem to miss her dad all summer. She was pretty sure Grandpa and Grandma wouldn't want to be apart that long.

"Well, try to keep it down. I have to get up early tomorrow; all the fish will be waiting for me," he said, laughing. Fishing was his passion. Beth couldn't imagine sitting out on the lake in the boat for hours on end the way he did. But she loved the delicious meals he brought home and appreciated that he always cleaned the fish before she had anything to do with them.

"What should we play tonight, Grandma?" Karina asked, as she helped put away the supper dishes.

"Well, let me see. How about canasta? You like that, don't you? We'll see what Elvira says about it, okay?"

"Okay, I hope she wants to. She gets so mad when I get the aces. I think it's funny," Karina said, with a devilish grin. "She's really nice though; I like her," she added.

Elvira was a widow who lived on the other side of old Pete. She had come to welcome Grandma and Grandpa the first day they arrived at the cottage. She and Grandma became fast friends and spent a lot of time together, especially when Grandpa was out fishing. Elvira had an old black Buick that had seen better days, and she drove like "a bat out of hell," Grandma said, but they often went into town together to shop. Karina loved going along. She would sit in the back seat and listen to the two of them talking non-stop. At times they would forget she was with them and she heard some things she was pretty sure she shouldn't have.

There was a tap-tap at the door and Elvira was inside.

"Come in," Grandma called from the kitchen.

"I'm in," Elvira called back, walking to the door of the kitchen. "Are you two ready to get beaten?" she asked, laughing.

"Not so fast there, Elvira," Grandma said, laughing too. "What shall we play? We're ready for you, whatever the game," she added, winking at Karina.

"What'll it be, Karina? You pick," Elvira said, digging into the enormous bag she hauled everywhere she went.

"How about canasta?" she offered.

"Canasta it is," Elvira said, pulling bottles of root beer from her bag.

"Beth, I'm assuming that you have some vanilla ice cream in that freezer of yours, because I've got my mind set on black cows later." It was the drink of choice on card night, root beer floats after a game or two.

"I certainly do have ice cream. I picked it up today, just for tonight," Grandma said.

"Mom, why don't you play, too?" Karina asked. Her mother usually read a book or sat down on the pier and smoked on these nights.

"Not tonight, Honey. I bought a new book in town today," she said.

"Oh, Mary Beth, your eyes are going to fall out you read so much. Why not have a game first," Elvira suggested.

"I hate canasta," Mary Beth pouted. "I'd rather read."

"Well, suit yourself," Grandma said, as she got the table ready for the game.

"I'll shuffle," Karina said.

# ~3~

Late in the afternoon, after a swim and an hour in the sun, Karin climbed the wooden stairs. She was thirsty. She must have fallen asleep because her shoulders felt burned. She lifted the strap of her bathing suit and saw the white line beneath it. "Oh, that ought to feel *real* good tonight," she said, aloud. When she was inside the house, she carefully rubbed lotion on the burned areas and scolded herself for not being more careful.

The phone rang just as she was washing the few dishes she had used for her supper. She dried her hands and answered it.

"Hello."

"Hi, Honey," he said. "How're you doing?"

"Hi, Brian. I'm fine. How are you?" She thought she sounded stiff and strange, but he didn't seem to notice.

"We're okay. I just wanted to check on you. Are you getting a lot done?"

"Ah . . . well, yes. Actually I'm having a bit of a rest, too. I've been so busy lately," she said.

"I know. I feel like I haven't seen you for weeks,

not days," he said.

"Is Kaitlin all right? Is she babysitting?"

"She's starting, three days a week for the Saunder's kids. Should keep her busy all summer."

"Is she okay, though?"

"Yes, Dear, she's fine," he answered.

"Well, give her my love and thanks for calling." She wondered if he had finished talking. She didn't know, but she wanted to hang up, now.

"Well, okay then. I'll call you tomorrow sometime. I love you, Karin."

"Me, too. Bye." She couldn't figure out what was wrong with her. She could hardly be civil to her own husband, and she hadn't even asked to talk to her daughter. She thought all she needed was some time away from them and the job, but the idea that it might be something else frightened her.

She found a box of pictures on the top shelf in Grandma's closet. She carefully took it down and tried to forget the phone call. She sat Indian style on Grandma's bed and opened the box. In it, she found lots of pictures of her and Sonny, her blonde hair always in braids and his, dark brown and cut in a crew-cut. They wore shorts with their shirts hanging out, and often their feet were bare. With their arms draped over each others shoulders they resembled a pair of contented beach-bums. She smiled as she looked through the photographs, remembering the fun they'd had then.

Sonny and Aunt Millie came up almost every other weekend. From what Karina heard, Aunt Millie didn't care too much for Uncle Bob. No one had actually *said* it, but she knew. Sometimes she would hear the grownups talking after they thought she was asleep. They would sit in the room with the wood burning stove those nights, because she and Sonny were sleeping on the daybed in the big room. He always went right to sleep, but she didn't and would sometimes lie awake even after the adults were in bed. It drove her crazy - being the only one awake.

She came across a picture of herself and Sonny down on the pier. He was holding up a small fish proudly, with a wide grin on his face.

~~~

"Hey, Karina. Do you know what a Muskie is?"

"No. What is it?"

"Well, I figured you didn't. It's a big fish, sorta' like a pike. You know what that is, don't you?"

"I guess so," she muttered, thoroughly bored with this conversation.

"Well, I heard that there's a humongous one living in the bay. I think we should go there today and try to catch him."

There was a point of land and a sandbar two lots south of their pier, and on the other side of that was a bay. They often went there just to sit and fish or play cards, and sometimes they took a lunch with them. It was a great place to spend the afternoon.

"Just exactly who told you this, Sonny?" she asked, very doubtful of his story.

"Old Pete said there's a Muskie in that bay that's at least fifty years old. Maybe a hundred!"

"Well, we'd better bring our lunch," she said. "Sounds like it could take awhile." This was the second year at the cottage. Sonny was twelve now and Karina eleven. They were still like kids, something their mothers were grateful for.

"Grandma, can we take our lunch out on the lake today?" Karina asked.

"Where out on the lake?" she wanted to know. The first year Grandpa had fastened a rope to the bow of the rowboat and tied it to the pier, so they could drift out the length of it. It was very long, but Grandpa knew where the lake got deep and made the rope just short of that, so they were safe. This year they were braver, and by now Grandpa had a new fiberglass boat and motor. Well, actually it was used, but Grandpa always said it was new to him. So the old wooden rowboat was always available.

"We want to go to the bay and fish," Sonny answered.

"That's okay, but don't go any farther, you hear? What do you want for lunch?" she asked.

Cheese sandwiches were made, and off they went, fishing for Muskellunge with lines and poles for bluegill.

"This fish is as big as a log, Karina. I'm not joking," Sonny told her, dropping the anchor when they were in the bay. "They lay on the bottom, so we have to attract him somehow. Maybe we should use a lure. Look and see if there's one in that tackle box," he instructed.

"What makes you think we can catch him if he's fifty years old, and no one has caught him yet?" she asked.

"Well, I just have a feeling. And I'm telling you if he takes the bait, you'll have to help me pull him in. He's huge, really huge!"

~~~

She smiled remembering for all Sonny's effort that day, they had caught one very small sunfish and Grandma had taken their picture with it. She continued looking through the pictures. There was one of her and Clare, her good friend from down the road. Her name was Clarice, but she preferred to be called Clare. She stayed four cottages down from them. It was a gravel road then and the girls would take long walks, picking berries, talking and telling secrets. "Ah, Clare, I wonder where you are now?" she murmured.

When she looked at the clock, it was nearly ten o'clock. She had been sitting there for hours. She got off the bed and stretched; her burned shoulders hurt. She put on more of the soothing cream that she found in the medicine cabinet. She would clean that out tomorrow, for it was filled with lots of jars and bottles that could be thrown away.

She got ready for bed and turned out the lights. Getting as comfortable as she could with her sore shoulders, she lay staring at the ceiling, pondering the value of this piece of real estate that she had inherited. The deed stated it was one hundred feet of lake front. It would be worth a lot of money today. She had smiled when she read what Grandpa had paid for it thirty years ago. He would be shocked to know its worth today.

Her grandparents had sold their house back home after the cottage was renovated and paid off the mortgage early. She yawned and wondered if she should sell it or keep it. If she kept it, would she ever find the time to come here and enjoy it? She carefully turned onto her side and went to asleep. This night, Clare filled her dreams.

~~~

"Grandma, where's Mom?" she asked, as she finished her breakfast in the big room.

"I think she's down at the lake," she answered. Grandma didn't like her daughter smoking in the cottage. She didn't like her smoking at all, but what could she say; she was, after all, a grown woman.

"I wonder if she would take Clare and me into town today. We could have lunch and just hang around."

"Well, run down and ask her. I could use a few things from the store, so you can use that as an excuse, if you want."

"Thanks, Gram," she said and ran out the door.

The girls were driven into town and would be picked up at three in the afternoon.

"We have four hours all to ourselves. This is great!" Clare said, excitedly. She was eleven now, a year younger than Karina. "Let's go to the drug store and get a Coke; then we can decide what we should do, okay?"

"Yes, let's," Karina said, and off they went. They drank Cokes and planned their day. First they tried on lots of clothes at the dry goods store until the clerk asked them if they had any intention of buying something. They told her of course they did, if they could find something that suited them. Then they put on their own clothes and left the store, laughing. The five and dime was next; that kept them busy awhile. The one movie theater in town was showing a stupid movie about a monster who lived in a swamp, but if they ran out of things to do, they would go see it.

"This is such a hick town, Karina. We have at least ten theaters back home," Clare announced. The girls lived in neighboring states back home, but had never visited each other there.

"Yeah, we have a few, too," Karina said. "But I sort of like this little hick town as you call it." Clare lived in a suburb of a very large city. Karina came from a much smaller town. They went back to the drug store for lunch and spent time at the cosmetic counter. Each applied different lipsticks from the samples, trying to find one that would look nice with Clare's red hair. They tired of that and decided to go to the stupid movie after all.

Clare was very curious about Sonny. "Why doesn't he come up more often? Don't you miss him? I think he's so cute! I wish he'd come this weekend," she said. "Clare, he doesn't come every weekend. It's usually every other weekend. I told you that," Karina said. Clare really made her mad about Sonny. He was *her* cousin and she didn't want to share him. She knew he could never like her the way boys like girls, but he was a boy, and she didn't want Clare in between them.

~4~

She missed the sunrise by hours this morning, but didn't care. She had slept well in spite of her sunburn. She had a vague sense of her old friend Clare when she woke. She thought perhaps she had dreamed about her, but remembered nothing. It must have been the pictures she had looked at the night before.

Today she would start sorting through her grandmother's things. The clothes would go to charity and many things would stay, if she decided to keep the property, that is. She tossed the thought around, weighing the pros and cons. She supposed she should discuss it with Brian. "Well, I am the realtor in the family, aren't I?" She asked herself and quickly put him out of her mind.

She had arrived at a figure as to the worth of the lake property, and it was mind boggling. She thought it would be quite a coup to sell it and make a small fortune, after never having invested a penny. Grandma had left stock and other investments to Karin's sister. She knew that Karol would have no interest in this property. She lived in New York in a high rise building that overlooked Central Park. Karin had visited her once and couldn't wait to get back home. She spent the night in her sister's apartment and listened to the sirens and traffic all night long. She wondered how her sister could stand it, but Karol loved it, and she told her sister often. She absolutely loved it.

As she went through her grandmother's things on Sunday, she thought about how simple and easy her life must have been. She was a wife to Grandpa and a mother to her kids. That didn't seem too hard. She did work at the nursery in town one summer, until Grandpa said he missed her at home. So she quit. Just like that - she quit.

Karin sorted through the first three drawers of the dresser and stacked the usable clothing neatly on the bed. When she opened the bottom drawer, she found her grandma's journals. She sat down on the bed and began to read. As she read, she remembered the baby her grandparents had lost. Their first born son had died at eighteen months old, and they were never exactly sure from what. He had simply gotten very sick one night with a high fever. They took him to the hospital, and he had died. Just died! She wondered how they had survived that. It was five years before they had another child, which was Karin's mother.

The journal explained. *Little Carl isn't feeling well today. He is very fussy and has no appetite. I will call Dr. O'Donald tomorrow*, Grandma had written. Then one week later: *Yesterday we buried little Carl. My heart has been torn out of my chest. His father hardly talks. His pain is unbear-*

*able, I know.*

Karin wondered how had they gotten past that, if in fact they ever had. The pages in the journal before his illness, spoke at length of Grandma's baby son: when his first tooth appeared, when he had learned to crawl and his first steps. She wrote about her home and Grandpa, too. That was her life. "Why are we not satisfied with this anymore?" she questioned, knowing that she wouldn't be; she loved her job, so much so, that she had never had the time to have another child. She regretted that now, or maybe just said it now, knowing she was too old. She knew that Brian had truly wanted more children, but she was the one who actually had to go through it all. She closed the journal and went down to the lake.

Sitting on the old bench, she stared into the water thinking about all the hours she had spent doing this over the years. She had loved every day she was here. When she was sixteen, she drove up on weekends when she could. Her mother was working then, so summers at the lake were over. Karina had a summer job, too, but still loved weekends here.

Sometimes she would bring a friend along, as Grandma had said everyone was welcome. Once or twice her mom and dad had driven up, too. Her dad went fishing with Grandpa, but he wasn't much of a fisherman. He preferred golf.

Suddenly she felt hungry. This was wonderful - she could eat when and what she wanted without worrying about her family. She ran up the steps to the house and dragged the grill out of the garage. She found charcoal and lighter fluid there, too. She'd bought ground chuck at the store, made hamburger patties out of the meat and frozen them. She had taken one out of the freezer earlier in the day. She threw together a salad and that was dinner. So much easier than at home.

Then it struck her! Maybe she wanted to be alone. "Do I want to be alone?" She asked herself. She had never articulated that thought before. She certainly didn't miss Brian or Kaitlin so far, and wondered if they felt the same. They sure didn't talk much anymore. She and Brian were both so busy with their jobs, and Kaitlin was just sort of *there*. She went to school and pretty much did her own thing. Now she was babysitting, Brian had told her, so she would be home even less this summer. That's the way life is nowadays; everyone is busy. If you're anyone at all, you're busy.

She poured a glass of chardonny and took it down to the lake. She wondered how Grandma did it; how it was that her husband and family were enough for her. She wondered why she didn't miss her own family. It had only been three days, but she was curious to know if Brian felt the same way, too. She hadn't talked to him today.

Thinking she should call home, she walked slowly up the steps to the house. The phone was ringing when she opened the screen door and she ran to answer it.

"Hello," she said.

"Hi, are you busy?" he asked.

"No, I just came up from the lake to call you."

"Do you live down by the lake?" he inquired. "Every time I call . . ."

"I love the lake; you know that," she said, rather shortly.

"Oh, I know, I just meant . . . how are you anyway? Do you need anything?" he asked.

"I'm fine and no, I don't need anything."

"Well, it's awfully quiet around here without you," he said, hoping that maybe she would say that she missed him a *little*.

"I'll be there in a week, and then it will be the same old stuff," she said.

"What's that suppose to mean?" he asked, truly puzzled.

"How is Kaitlin?" she continued, ignoring his question.

"She's fine. She likes her babysitting job and loves the money," he said, quietly. "Well, I'll let you go then. I love you."

"Me, too. Bye," was all she could say.

She went out to the garage to put away the grill. They never left it outside, ever since someone dumped it all over the driveway. She put her car in as well and pulled down the overhead door, making sure it was locked. They had never gotten around to installing a garage door opener. For some reason, Grandpa thought it was a waste of money.

"I pity the man who can't open his own garage door," he would grumble if someone suggested how nice it would be. Grandma never drove much and not at all after Grandpa died, or she probably would have put one in for sure.

Back in the house, she locked the doors and went

into Grandma's room to look at more pictures and read more of her journal. There were so many pictures; she didn't remember Grandma taking so many.

A picture of herself and Patsy sitting in the adirondack chairs over looking the lake took her back to the age of eleven again. They were sitting in the chairs drinking Kool-aid in tall glasses with straws. They both had on sunglasses and looked deep in thought. They didn't know they were being photographed.

~~~

Patsy was quite a character and Karina was fascinated by her. She was two years older than Karina, but acted as if she were about eighteen. She was an only child and her parents were divorced. Every year that she and her mother came up to the cottage, they brought with them a different man. Grandma thought it was appalling, to say the least, and was always grateful when Patsy's stay had ended. Karina heard lots of conversation on that subject, when they thought she was asleep.

It didn't seem to bother Patsy one iota. As long as Mother's men, as she called them, treated her okay, she didn't care what they did.

"But where is your Dad? Do you ever see him?" Karina asked one day as they sat in the rowboat.

"I've never seen him, actually," Patsy said, in a haughty way, hoping to shock her young companion a bit.

"But why would you never see him?" she asked, thoroughly confused. "He isn't dead, is he?"

"No, he isn't dead. I honestly don't think my mother knows who he is."

Now more confused than before, Karina was trying hard to figure out how that could be. She knew how babies were made, of course. After all she was eleven years old, but couldn't comprehend how a person could not know who they did *that* with? She wondered whether or not it was possible that someone could do that to you while you were sleeping. That was a frightening thought. She didn't want to ask Patsy to explain, for fear she would look stupid.

"Why are you so quiet, Karina? It happens all the time, you know," she told her.

"Oh, I was just thinking," she said, feeling her face get red. She hated when she blushed. She turned her face away from Patsy and wondered *what* happens all the time. She thought maybe she could ask Sonny when he came up for the weekend, if she dared.

She never got up the nerve to ask Sonny, but after many weeks of puzzling over what Patsy told her, she approached her grandma.

"Whatever made you ask that kind of question, Karina?" Grandma asked.

"Well, Patsy said that she didn't think her mom knew who her dad was."

"I should have known," Grandma said. "That girl is not good for you, child. I'm glad she's only here one week!" Then she asked if Karina knew how a woman became pregnant.

"Yes, I know," she answered, quietly. Then Grandma proceeded.

"If a girl drops her pants for every guy who comes along, as I'm sure her mother did, and still does, and then she gets pregnant, how on earth would she know who the baby belonged to? You save yourself, Karina. Find a nice man and it will be special, not just a roll in the hay." Karina felt her face redden. She really wished she hadn't asked.

# ~5~

Tuesday morning Karin woke to pounding rain. She jumped out of bed and closed the window. It was too early to get up, but she went into the big room to look at the lake. The light on the pier went on automatically at dusk, so she was able to see. The lake looked ominous; it was so rough and choppy. She shuddered and remembered the time when she and Grandpa were out fishing and a storm came up out of nowhere, catching them off guard. She had been scared to death, but Grandpa was calm and reassuring as he covered her with a rain parka he kept under the seat. The waves were so rough that the motor was of no use. He had manned the oars as best he could, and they had waited it out. It didn't last long, but she never forgot how frightened she had been watching the lightning and cowering when the thunder crashed. She padded barefoot back to her bed and curled up on her side. Feeling very safe, she slept.

When she woke again the rain had stopped, but the leaves on the trees were drooping, laden with moisture. It was still gray out, but the sun was trying to peek through the clouds and the birds were beginning to sing. She opened the windows in the big room, inhaling the freshly cleaned air. It smelled wonderful.

She filled the coffee pot and turned it on. When it finished dripping, she took a mug of the fresh brew out to the big porch facing the road and sat in Grandma's rocking chair. The huge pine trees were wet and heavy; the lower branches nearly touched the ground.

She rocked slowly and sipped her coffee, feeling very content. She didn't miss anything. She had been so gung ho after she was awarded salesperson of the month, that she'd nearly killed herself trying to do it again. Now she couldn't care less. She thought about that awhile, deciding it had been an ego trip for sure, and that's when things started falling apart at home. There, she had said it. She had admitted it, finally, to herself anyway. "What the hell happened to me?" she asked herself. "How could an award be so important?" She had worked very hard for it, that's how.

She shifted in her chair and thought about going in and getting dressed, but didn't. This little part of the world was perfect today. It was freshly washed and gleaming. The sun was shining now, and a cool breeze caressed her face. She thought about her husband and wondered if she had neglected him. None of the women she knew would think she had. He was forty-two years old and a senior executive in an advertising firm, a very satisfying position with a salary to match. What more could he want? She was the one who was just getting started on the ladder of success. She didn't understand, if it was success, why she didn't feel better. Pondering this, she caught a glimpse of old Pete's car coming down the road. She quickly went into the house before he drove by. She didn't want to be caught sitting outside in Grandma's old chenille robe.

~~~

Dressed and ready for the day, she planned to go into town to do a little shopping. She would buy her husband and daughter a gift. The thought of doing that made her feel good, and she hoped she would be able to find something suitable.

What she found was more than suitable; it was perfect - a soft knit golf shirt for Brian and a light weight, white cardigan sweater for Kaitlin. She was pleased with her purchases and even bought wrapping paper for them. She couldn't remember the last time she had bought either one of them a present for no reason other than she cared. She'd been so busy . . . .

While in town, she had asked about charities where she could take Grandma's clothes. She was given a few names and wrote them down. Back home, she put the list on the counter in the kitchen and decided to complete the job of going through the clothes today. She would take everything into town within a few days.

She thought, in the back of her mind, that she very much wanted to keep the lake house, but couldn't bring herself to dwell on it seriously, yet. She had lots of thoughts *in the back of her mind* just now, thoughts about her husband, her daughter, and her life. She wondered why she couldn't concentrate on them. "Is it because I'd have to take a good look at myself?" she questioned. That was as far as she got with thinking and busied herself in Grandma's closet.

There were only a few dresses hanging on padded hangers. Life at the lake house had always been casual, and Grandma usually wore pants and a shirt. If it got really hot, she would put on shorts, but she preferred long pants. At the back of the closet she found the dress her grandmother had worn for Grandpa's funeral and then one more time for Karin's mother's. It was carefully wrapped in a white sheet. So much had happened to Grandma in those last ten years of her life, and much of it wasn't good.

She lost her husband, another one of her children and her remaining daughter was divorced and in yet another unhappy marriage.

"Poor Grandma," Karin said softly to no one.

She remembered Grandpa's funeral so well. It was very sad. He had died so quickly that no one had any time to prepare for it, as if one could prepare for something like that. Grandma said she was grateful he didn't suffer, but that was the only consolation. She was lost without him. She had been very brave that day, Karin remembered, keeping her little family close to her side throughout the day. They buried him in the small cemetery just outside of the town where they shopped. Grandma had gotten her stone at that time too, so it would match his. Her name and date of birth were engraved on it with a space for her date of death. It always gave Karin a strange feeling to see Grandma's tombstone, when she was standing right beside her. They would go to the grave to visit Grandpa every time Karin was at the lake.

"Old Pete takes me to visit Grandpa's grave sometimes when we go into town together," Grandma told Karin one day. "He's a good old soul," she added.

Old Pete had been at the funeral, Karin remembered. He sat way in back so as not to intrude on the family. She had made a point of personally inviting him back to the lake house for the lunch they had planned. He had hesitated at first, but she insisted that he would be missed if he didn't. No one knew him well, but somehow, he had always been part of life at the lake.

~~~

She took a break for lunch, looking over the names of the charities she had written down and decided she would give the nicest things to the County Rest Home. The residents there had little or nothing. She hoped it would make the women feel better if they had something nice to wear. She would also take her jewelry there. Grandma didn't have much, just some earrings and necklaces that were pretty.

She was smiling as she ate lunch and decided she would visit the rest home first to check out the place and the resident women. Maybe she could find a special old lady who would appreciate her grandma's things. She rinsed out her glass and placed it in the sink with the breakfast dishes. Back in the bedroom, she uncovered the funeral dress and remembered her own mother's death.

~~~

Karin stopped at the nurse's station before entering her mother's room.

"Hello, how may I help you?" a pretty nurse looked up from her charting and asked. This was a new nurse, or at least Karin had never seen her before today.

"My mother, Mary Beth, in room three-sixty. How is she doing?"

"Well, the night nurse said that she had a pretty quiet night. I've been taking care of her today, and so far, I've only medicated her one time for pain. She seems fairly comfortable, so far," she said, smiling.

"May I go in?" Karin asked the nurse.

"Of course, and please let me know if she needs anything. My name is Beverly," she told her. Karin nodded her thanks and went down the corridor to her mother's room. It was dark, the blinds were closed. She looked as though she were asleep.

"Hi, Karina," her mother said, softly. She had refused to drop the "a" on her daughter's name.

"I thought you were sleeping," Karin said.

"Oh, I've been dozing on and off all morning. Why don't you open the blinds and let some of that sunshine in?" Karin did so and looked at the cards on the window sill.

"You've gotten a lot of cards, Mom. Some really pretty ones, too," she said, reading a few of them. "These are so nice. Has Dad been here today?" Her dad was having a hard time with her mother's illness.

"No, not yet. He'll probably stop in after work," she said. Karin wondered how long he stayed, but didn't ask. He had no one and nothing to go home to, but he never stayed with his wife very long. She thought it was strange, but could never recall them fighting or not getting along well. She didn't know how could he just leave her here, and why it didn't make her mother mad.

"I think Brian and Kaitlin will come with me tomorrow. Would you like that, Mom? She misses you and doesn't really understand what's happening."

Her mother had an inoperable, malignant tumor on her liver. They had operated, but simply closed her up again, as there was nothing they could do. The tumor had invaded a major blood vessel which made any excising impossible. That had been six weeks ago and the prognosis was bleak.

"We will keep her comfortable and as pain free as possible," the doctor had told them. It was all they could do. She had been home with a nurse coming every day, until one week ago.

"Yes, I always love to see them, you know that, her mother had said. "As for Kaitlin not understanding, don't you think maybe that's up to you, Karina? She is seven years old after all; she knows what death is."

Her mother was so . . . what was the word? Stoic? No, that was too harsh. She started to cry and took her mother's hand. "Mother, I don't know how you do this. Aren't you mad as hell at something or someone? It isn't fair!" she said, blowing her nose.

"Sweetheart, what's fair? That isn't how life works. Do you think these things are meted out by some being, either randomly or with intent? You can't

think that. This kind of thing happens, that's all."
Karin put her head down on the bed next to her
mother and hoped that she had inherited some of
her mettle.

Karol had flown in from New York and stayed
for one week but had to return home. She would
come back when the end was near, which wouldn't
be long. Grandma, however, nearly lived at the hospital. They could hardly drag her out of there. She
stayed in a nearby motel because it was close to the
hospital. Karin had begged her to stay with her at
her home, but she wanted to be closer to her dying
daughter.

Grandma was absolutely devastated to think that
one of her girls would be dead before her. She would
sit at her daughter's bedside and silently think of
her baby son all those years ago, and her beloved
husband. She didn't think that any of this was fair,
and wondered if it was some sort of a test. She was
happy to give her Mary Beth comfort. She would
rub her back, read the paper to her, or just sit quietly by the bed.

Karin's dad had told his mother-in-law again and
again how much he appreciated her being there.

"I'm just no good at that sort of thing, Beth," he
told Grandma when Mary Beth had first gotten sick.
Grandma didn't understand but was glad he didn't
mind her being there.

"Who *is* good at this sort of thing?" Grandma
asked herself aloud.

The call came at three o'clock in the morning. It
was the night nurse. Brian answered the phone.
"Yes, she's right here," he said, handing the receiver

to his wife. He helped her sit up in bed and put his arm around her. She cleared her throat before speaking.

"Hello. Yes, this is Karin. I see. We'll be there in thirty minutes," she said and gave him the phone.

"She's dying now. They don't expect her to live until morning. Oh, Brian, I don't want her to die," she said, crying.

"I know. I know," he said, patting her back. "You get up and do what you have to do. I'll call Cindy next door and ask her to come over so Kaitlin isn't alone. Do you want to tell her or should I?" he asked.

Oh, God! How was she going to tell her daughter that her grandma was dying right now? They had talked about it a lot, so she had prepared her, but she didn't want it to happen now. She wanted her mother to live to be an old lady like Grandma, but it wasn't to be.

They arrived at the hospital before she was gone. Karin sat beside the bed and took her hand.

"I love you, Mother. I love you so." She whispered it over and over. She had heard somewhere that hearing is the last sense to leave the body at the time of death. She wanted to be sure her mother knew. Her dad was on the other side of the bed. He looked as if he wasn't sure what to do. Brian had gone to pick up Grandma. She watched her mother's last breaths. They were shallow now and uneven; it was nearly over. Grandma and Brian had gotten there just before her last breath. Grandma was inconsolable. Karin's dad had hung onto her and sobbed quietly. Karol was on her way; in fact, she had been in the air when her mother died.

When the papers were signed and arrangements made, they went home, taking Grandma with them. They sat at the kitchen table, drinking coffee, waiting for their daughter to awaken. When Kaitlin woke, her eyes were red. She had cried quietly in her bed after Karin had told her they were going to the hospital and why.

At the funeral, Kaitlin clutched a lace handkerchief that her grandmother had given her and went up to the coffin alone, whispering something to her that no one heard. Then she stood on her tip toes and kissed her grandmother's forehead and put a rose beside the body. She sat between her mother and her great-grandmother at the service, feeling sad for them both.

Aunt Millie was there with her second husband. Grandma had never cared for him and, to this day, resented the divorce from Uncle Bob, who sat in the back, apart from the family. Sonny sat with his wife and kids. It had been a difficult time.

# ~6~

Karin looked at her watch and was satisfied with what she had accomplished since lunch. The boxes she had gotten at the grocery store were neatly packed with clothes and the shoes were wrapped in white paper. She had placed the costume jewelry in a small box and tucked it in with the clothes. It would all be taken tomorrow.

It was nearly time for dinner, but she couldn't think of a thing to eat, so she went down to the lake and settled herself on the bench. It would be fun to go out in that old rowboat one more time, she thought, remembering the fun she and Sonny had.

She heard a boat approaching and turned to see who it was. A man was waving to her as he turned off the motor.

"Hello, there. Are you staying at the cottage up there?" he asked.

"Yes, it belongs to me," she answered, curious now.

"Well, I don't mean to bother you, but I've caught way too many fish today. Would you like some? I've got a few crappie and a couple of bluegill. I've even cleaned them," he added.

"Well, how could I refuse? Cleaning them is the part I don't care for."

He maneuvered his boat alongside the pier and stood, extending his hand to her.

"My name is Philip. I'm staying three cottages down with my wife and kids."

"Nice to meet you, Philip. I'm Karin," she said, shaking his hand.

"My wife saw you sitting here and told me to ask you if you could help us eat some of these fish. The kids don't eat much. They're afraid they'll find bones," he said, laughing.

"Well, I'd be delighted. I was just wondering what I would fix for dinner tonight. Now you've solved that for me, and I thank you."

"My pleasure," he said, sitting down and starting his motor. "I hope you enjoy the fish," he called to her as he drove away.

Picking up the little bundle of fish, she started up the stairs. "What a nice surprise!" she said to no one.

Back in the house, she got out Grandma's cast iron frying pan and found the cooking oil in the cupboard. She was leery about the flour though, hating those little bugs that sometimes find their way in it. She carefully sifted the flour she would need and found none of the little critters.

She hadn't had fresh fish in a long time. As the oil was heating, she floured the little pieces of fish and started to fry them. They smelled wonderful!

Brian would be home in an hour. She wanted to call him tonight. She made a salad, with some bread.

That would be plenty. There were quite a few fish here, but they were small. She didn't think she would have any trouble eating them all. One week ago, she would be trying to determine the amount of calories in this meal. That was a relief, too. She hadn't thought about dieting all week. She sat at the table by the window and enjoyed her surprise dinner, savoring every morsel.

She was rinsing her plate when the phone rang.

"Hello," she said, grabbing a towel to dry her hands.

"Well, hello to you," he said.

"Oh, Brian, I wanted to call you today. Aren't you home early?"

"I'll hang up and you can call me," he teased.

"Oh, don't be silly," she said, laughing.

"Yes, I'm home early. I just felt like coming home. I wish you were here, though."

"Ah, you're sweet. I'll be home soon. Tomorrow is already Wednesday. Only four days to go," she said. She sounded much more like her old self.

"Well, how are you doing up there? Getting everything done?" he asked.

"I've gotten all Grandma's things together, and I'm going to take them to the County Rest Home in town tomorrow; so that's done. I'm not sure about the house. If I keep it, most of the things will stay, but if I don't, I'll have to have a sale I guess," she said, not asking him what he thought.

"Well, I'm sure you'll do the right thing, Dear," he told her.

"Is Kaitlin there?" she asked.

"She's at a friend's, so I'm on my own for dinner," he said, sounding a bit lonely.

"You'll never guess what I had for dinner," she said.

"What?"

"A neighbor, three doors down brought me some fish he caught today. They were delicious! He even cleaned them!"

"Who is he?" he hesitated. "How do you know him?"

"I don't know him, silly. His wife saw me down on the pier and told him to ask me if I wanted some fish because they couldn't eat all of them."

"Oh, I see," he said sounding relieved.

"You didn't think I had a man here for dinner, now, did you?" she teased.

"Well, of course I didn't," he said, a little too firmly. He sounded as though he truly missed her and was maybe a bit jealous there for a moment.

"I'll let you go. Call if you need anything. You are staying until Sunday then, right?"

"Yes, I'll be home Sunday afternoon sometime. I'll call you before I leave so you'll know when to expect me, okay?"

"Yeah, do that. Okay, I love you. Bye," he said.

"Bye, I love you, too, Brian," she said, softly. He was smiling when he hung up the phone. She sounded much more like the old Karin.

One more trip down to the lake, and she would call it a day. She picked up her glass of wine that she hadn't finished with her dinner and went out the door. She carefully made her way down the wooden steps to the pier. The evening was beautiful. She sat on the bench and sipped her chardonny.

She watched the boats on the lake and thought about her husband. She missed him a little - maybe more than a little. She thought she would get up early tomorrow and watch the sunrise. She'd only done it once so far. It was so nice not to have to get up at certain time and be somewhere. Maybe she would keep the house and come here every summer alone. Alone? She drew up her knees and put her arms around her legs. Suddenly she wished Brian was here with her, but then thought that they would probably have to be doing something if he was. She didn't want to do a thing except sit here and watch the lake.

When it started to get dark, she took her time going up the stairs and into the house. Inside, she realized that she had not turned on the television since she arrived. She picked up the remote and pushed the button. The evening news was starting. No wonder she hadn't missed it. A plane crash, a school shooting, and a child molester on the loose were the news flashes tonight. She stood in the middle of the big room and watched. The school shooter was fourteen years old. Had she heard that correctly? Surely she couldn't have.

"Oh, dear God," she whispered and turned it off, feeling stunned. She had heard it correctly. The shooter was fourte, not much older than Kaitlin. How could this be? There was so much violence in the world today; it wasn't even funny. She turned off the lights and went into the bathroom to get ready for bed. "It's so different up here," she said to her reflection in the mirror. "A person can live quite peacefully and focus on what's important," she decided as she loaded her toothbrush with toothpaste.

"And what is important to you, Mrs. Brian Parker?" she asked herself as she brushed her teeth. Pondering that, she turned off the bathroom light and turned on the night light. It was so dark here, no street lights, and tonight the moon was only a curved slit of light in the blackened sky. She went into Grandma's room and opened up the bed, thinking about what she had asked herself in the mirror. She picked up Grandma's journal and began reading.

*Today I'm almost sure that I am pregnant again. I'm so happy I could scream! I don't want to tell Carl until I'm positive. I could not bear to disappoint him in this way. I will go to the doctor in the morning for an examination, then I will know for sure. I secretly pray for a boy to replace little Carl, but I know no one could ever take his place. I will be happy with whatever the good Lord sees fit to give us.*

The next entry:
*I am pregnant for sure! The doctor told me so. I am two and one half months along. I can't write much today as I want to make Carl's favorite dinner, baked pork chops and dressing. Tonight will be special.*

This pregnancy would be Karin's mother. It was exciting, even after all these years. She wondered if women were this happy about a pregnancy today. There were many things to consider now, like how much time one could take off from work, and where would one place a newborn when the mother goes back to work? Grandma didn't have those problems. She stayed home with the children, and Grandpa worked to support them all.

When Kaitlin was born, Karin was a full-time mom. She didn't regret that for a moment. She thought it probably was the one thing she had done right. She hadn't looked for work until Kaitlin was in school. She thought briefly about why she hadn't had more children. She pushed her reading glasses up on her head and leaned back against the pillow. Those were the good old days, for sure. She had been home with her baby. She hadn't missed a thing. Everything Kaitlin did, Karin was there to see and then could tell Brian when he came home from work. There was nothing so bad about that, but it seemed that no one wanted to do that today, no one she knew, anyway.

She'd had some close neighbors then who had little kids, too, and they would get together at one of their houses for coffee. They would visit and the kids would play. In the summer months, they would fill a little plastic pool for the kids and have iced tea in someone's back yard. Again she wondered why she hadn't had more kids.

She put her glasses on and read some more.

*Carl is ecstatic! It is so good to see him laugh. He hasn't been the same since little Carl passed away. He loved his dinner and talked about the baby all the while we did the dishes. I'm so grateful I have made him happy. He is such a good husband. I could not ask for more.*

Karin smiled and closed the journal. What a wonderful thing her grandparents had! She turned out the light and curled up on her side; then sat up quickly and set the alarm. She didn't want to miss the sunrise tomorrow. She cuddled down under the covers and thought about her grandparents. She realized that she did have what her grandma had had. A good husband and a wonderful daughter. Only one child, but she really was a great kid. Karin was beginning to miss her little family, and wondered how she had overlooked the importance of them. She felt like an idiot. She thought that maybe anyone could sell a house, but questioned how many people could take care of a family and keep them close. Grandma had done that so well. She went to sleep with Grandma in her thoughts.

# ~7~

The alarm clock buzzed quite awhile before she realized what it was. She was dreaming about work. She was showing a house that was an absolute dump, and the people looking at the house were either stupid or didn't understand English because they just kept staring at her. Then the doorbell was ringing, and no one moved. They just stared. She started for the door and woke. She reached for the clock and pushed in the button.

"What a weird dream," she whispered to herself, happy that it was a dream. The house was so awful. No one would have been able to sell it.

She got out of bed and went to the kitchen to start the coffee, then back to the bedroom to slip into her watching-the-sunrise clothes, as she called them. She opened some windows and let in the fresh air. It always smelled so good here.

"I love this place," she said, aloud, thinking about if that meant she had decided to keep it. She still didn't know. The coffee pot was quiet. It had finished brewing. She filled a mug and went out into the yard. It was very still at this time of morning.

The birds were just starting to chirp. She made her way down the steps to the pier and sat on the bench. She was just in time to see this beautiful spectacle that happened every single day and never lost its beauty. She sipped her coffee and saw her little part of the world wake. She never tired of watching this spectacular sight. Soon the diehard fishermen began to appear on the water. "The fish bite most at the break of day," she had heard over and over again. If it was true or not, she didn't know.

The water was crystal clear, and she saw a school of minnows disappear under the pier. She stood and waited for the tiny fish to reappear on the other side. It reminded her of how she and Sonny had tried to catch them in a net and that it wasn't easy. The whole group would dart sideways with lightning speed and swim away to avoid the net. It was impossible to catch them. She finished her coffee and slowly climbed the stairs. The sun was warm on her back. It would be another beautiful day.

In the house, she poured more coffee and took it into the bedroom. The curtains were blowing softly. She had such a sense of peace. "Maybe I will keep the house," she murmured. "But the money would be great." She needed to think about that. She wondered when money had become so important to her. It never was before. Brian was a good provider. He always had been. Making mega-bucks, as they say, had never been a priority, but when she was awarded sales person of the month and had gotten that big commission check, the bug had bitten her. She remembered that she didn't cash it for a week or so, looking at it often and showing her husband.

She thought it was stupid now. He never did that, and he made a lot of money, compared to her anyway. When he got a big check, he would come home and show it to her and say, "Now you can get . . .," something she had been wanting.

She began making the bed, thinking about that big check and likened it to a slippery slope. She hadn't been able to stop; she had wanted more. It seemed embarrassing to her now, as though a person's worth could be measured in money. Brian had never been like that. "What happened to me?" she whispered.

She picked out the clothes she would wear today and went into the bathroom to shower. Shampooing her hair, she wondered if she had been doing anything right lately.

Dressed and ready, she ate breakfast and began putting the boxes of clothes into the car. She tried to think of how she would go about getting rid of the furniture in the house, if she sold it. "Could I sell it furnished?" she asked herself. "Probably not," she answered. She thought she could if it were a cottage, but it was a home now, and whoever bought it would more than likely have their own things. The furnishings were nice, maybe not her taste exactly, but nice. All the old cottage stuff was long gone now and probably in an antique shop with a price tag five or six times what Grandpa had paid.

She made sure the doors were locked and turned off the coffee pot, then went through the small breezeway to the garage. Grandpa had the garage built on the kitchen side of the cottage. The pantry had been taken out to make way for a door. A screened passageway led to the garage. She remembered how Grandma didn't want to give up her pantry. There had been much discussion about that. Grandpa insisted it was the best way to do it and eventually put more cupboards in the kitchen, so everyone was happy.

She drove into town with the windows down. It felt so good. The air was fresh and clean, not polluted like it was back home. She arrived at the rest home, parking as close as she could, making it easy to carry in the boxes. She was treated like a celebrity when she told the woman at the desk why she was there.

"You have no idea how much these women will appreciate your grandmother's things! It will surely brighten their day, believe me. Some of the women don't have much and some don't even have family close by," she explained, "and gracious no, you don't have to carry in the boxes. I will page Henry, our maintenance man."

"May I look around a bit?" Karin asked.

"Of course. Make yourself at home. Most of the residents are in the common room now. It's down the hall on the left," she told her.

Karin heard the woman page Henry as she made her way down the hall. She stayed outside the room and looked in through the glass doors. A few of the people were in wheelchairs, and they all appeared to be well cared for. Some of the women looked to be Grandma's size and Karin hoped they would like the clothes. She went back to the desk where Henry was waiting and took him out to her car. She carried the smaller boxes in against his wishes.

"You shouldn't be lifting that now, Ma'am! I can do it," he said.

"Oh, these aren't very heavy, Henry. I expected to carry all of them in, so I thank you," she said.

After that job was done, she took a drive around to the other side of the lake. It was still quite early and she hadn't been over there in years. Grandpa used to take them there often. There was a certain spot where they could see their own pier light after dark. It was small and hard to see, but Grandpa swore it was his light. Afterward they would go to the drive-in for old fashioned ice cream that tasted so good they would lick their cones slowly and make them last until they got back to the cottage. She remembered those days so well now.

It was such a beautiful day. She drove around the entire lake, passing some very old, elegant homes. She tried to estimate their value. They were quite old, but in very good shape.

She cut across the highway and went to the cemetery where her grandparents were buried. Grandma's grave was fresh, and her stone was not yet engraved. She would call and check on that before she went home. From the cemetery she went into town to have lunch at the drug store, where she and Clare hung out all those years ago. It had changed some, but still offered small town fare with its lunch counter and stools; that's what she liked about it. She settled herself on one of the stools and waited for the girl in the uniform and matching headband to take her order.

"I'd like a grilled cheese sandwich and a chocolate malt, please," she told her. "Calories be damned!" she muttered to herself. She was on vacation. It had been some time since she had a lunch like this. She wondered as she ate what she would do with the rest of the day. She thought a swim would be nice, and she would need it after this malt, but it tasted so good.

She paid for her lunch and left a gracious tip for the girl, then browsed through the store, picking up a few items she needed and took them up to the checkout counter. She thought about supper and stopped at the grocery store. Maybe she would get some steak, a potato or two and sour cream. She reminded herself that she was on vacation. To her surprise, she had several things in her cart when she went to check out, but she figured that she did have three and a half more days.

At two o'clock in the afternoon she got back to the house. She put away the food and changed into her swim suit. She took Grandma's journal, a towel, some sunscreen and a can of soda down to the lake. She had nothing to do until her stomach told her it was dinner time.

She was still reading Grandma's first journal, or at least the first one she had found. It began when Grandma and Grandpa married. Karin wondered if she had kept a journal as a girl. How fascinating this was to have her grandmother's life chronicled in this way. Her current journal had been lying on the night stand. The rest she found tied together with a wide grosgrain ribbon in the bottom drawer of the dresser. Karin would keep and treasure these writings, forever. She marveled at her grandmother's penmanship. The letters were neat and tiny, not unlike her stitches were whenever she mended something.

She read quickly up to the point of her own mother's birth.

*This baby is like a miracle!* Grandma had written. *She is very good and nurses well. When she isn't wet or hungry, she sleeps. She is a joy for sure. Her name is Mary Beth and it becomes her.*

Every page was full of her little daughter's early life. Karin wondered if her mother had ever read it. She continued reading.

*Mary Beth is taking her first steps and is everywhere. Her father will spoil her rotten, he is so thrilled with her. It's a good thing he works all day. It gives me a chance to 'unspoil' her. I would not have it any other way however. I have not seen my husband this happy in a long time.*

Karin smiled when she read that part. She wondered when being an at home mother became something women were much too smart to do? She had the feeling again that almost anyone could sell a house, but wondered if just anyone could raise a child. It seemed to her now, at this age, that to bring up a child to be a decent, intelligent human being, the person doing it would have to be pretty darn smart. She silently lamented not having had more kids.

She was getting hot now and thought how cool the lake would be. She slowly entered the water, getting used to the chill a little at a time. "Never swim alone," she remembered Grandpa saying. So when she swam by herself, she didn't go out where it was over her head. She just wanted to cool off a bit. It felt wonderful. She floated on her back and squinted her eyes at the sun.

"Oh, I love this place so much," she said, aloud. "Does that mean I'll keep it?" she asked. "Hmm, don't know for sure," she said, answering her own question. She stayed in the water watching some kids playing a few piers down. They were having so much fun, shrieking and splashing as they floated around in their little inner tubes. She had always loved doing that very thing.

She got out of the lake and toweled off a little, then sat on the bench to wait for her suit to dry. She stuck out her legs and realized she had gotten a tan while she was here. Usually she looked like Casper because she had no time for sunning. She gathered her things and climbed the wooden steps up to the house, wondering how many times she had been up and down these stairs in her life.

# ~8~

The phone was ringing when she entered the house. She ran to grab it, not knowing how long it had been ringing.

"Hello," she said.

"Well, hello to you, too! Were you sitting by the phone waiting for my call?" her sister Karol asked.

"No, why? Karol! How are you?" she said all at once.

"Well, it barely rang twice and you answered. And I'm fine thank you. How are you doing?" She hadn't talked to her sister since Grandma's funeral.

"I'm doing okay. I just walked up from the lake and heard the phone."

"So, what's going on? Are you selling the house? You'll make a killing, you know! And what's up with you? I called your house first. Why the devil are you up there all alone?" she asked. Her sister never minced words.

"I have to take care of Grandma's things, you know," she said, defensively.

"Oh, like what, putting Grandma's clothes in a bag and taking them to the Goodwill? What's there to do?"

"There are a few more things to do than that, Karol," she said, patiently, "and I wanted to come up alone. I'm trying to figure out a lot of stuff," she said, surprising herself by revealing that.

"Are you okay? What can't you figure out?"

Karol had never given her life much thought. She just plowed through everything that happened to her and she was happy. Karin was more introspective and analyzed everything, especially herself.

"Well, for one thing, I'm not sure I want to sell this house," she said.

"So, don't sell it. How can that be a problem? God, Karin, you worry too much, you know it?"

"Yeah, I know. How are Ralph and the boys?" she asked, hoping to change the subject.

"Oh, they're fine. The kids are hardly ever home. Ralph's all paranoid because he's getting gray hair," she said, laughing.

"Tell him it makes him looked distinguished."

"I tried that. He said, 'Bull shit, it makes me look old.' He'll get over it; everyone does. Well, little sister, I'll let you go. Write or call sometime, okay? And let me know what you decide to do with that house."

"I will, and thanks for calling. Say 'hi' to everyone for me. Bye, Karol."

"Bye, Karina," and she hung up.

"Ugh, I hate when she calls me that," she said to no one. "And that's exactly why she does it."

She opened the fridge; it was time to start dinner. She didn't think a nice man would deliver it again tonight. Closing the door of the fridge, she decided that steak with a baked potato and salad would taste good. She would shower first and then call home. Someone would be there by then.

She thought about her sister as she towel dried her hair. Looking in the mirror, she wondered if two siblings could be more different than they were. Karol was tall and exuded a sense of confidence, even as a little kid, that Karin would kill for. She was never a showoff, nor was she arrogant. She was simply comfortable in her own skin. Karin had developed confidence with age, as most folks do, but not without consciously working at it.

She blew her hair dry and put on clean clothes, then called home. No one answered, so she left a message at the beep. She took the grill out of the garage and brought it to the back yard. Actually it was what she thought of as the back, because it faced the lake. She and Grandma always called it that. The road was in the front, they figured, but she could still hear her grandparents arguing about it. She lit the coals and went back inside. Pouring a glass of wine, she wondered if her sister would ever drink white wine with a steak. They lived in different worlds. The salad was made and the potato was cooking, so she sat down by the window with Grandma's journal to wait for the coals to get hot. If she kept the house, she would invest in a gas grill for sure.

She found her place in the book and continued to read. It was all about her mother, everything the little girl did was recorded. She hoped her mother had read this. It was so interesting. When she got to the place where her mother was one and a half years old, tears came to her eyes.

*I know this is silly, but I'm terrified that some-*
*thing will happen to my Mary Beth now that she*
*is eighteen months old. I get up several times in the*
*night to check on her and she's always okay, but*
*I can't forget little Carl. I know it has nothing to*
*do with this child, but it still haunts me so! I tell*
*Carl this and he says, "Oh, Lizzie Beth, stop that*
*now", and gives me a hug.*

Karin wiped her eyes and thought that some
wounds must never completely heal.

The coals looked grey; it was time to cook. Her
steak turned out just the way she liked it. She was
a little surprised, as Brian always cooked the steaks
on the grill at home. She cleaned up after herself
and took her wine outside. She sat in one of the old
adirondak chairs at the end of the yard. She did-
n't feel like going down to the pier tonight. The view
up here was breathtaking! It seemed she could see
for miles. It was a beautiful evening again. The
crickets were chirping now, and soon the fireflies
would be showing their luminous rear ends. She put
her head back on the chair and let her mind drift
a little. She felt at peace; her belly was full and all
was well in this little part of the world.

"Oh, there you are," she heard someone say. She
must have dozed off. Straightening up in the chair
she looked over her shoulder. It was Pete.

"Hi, Pete. I think I dozed off for a minute. I did-
n't hear you," she said.

"I hope I didn't scare you. I was just out walking and remembered you would only be here until

Sunday, so I thought I'd stop and say hello."

"Come sit with me. It's so nice of you to stop. Would you like a glass of wine, Pete?" she asked.

"You wouldn't happen to have a cold beer, would you?" he asked, shyly.

"No, I don't. I'm here alone, and I don't drink beer. I'm sorry."

"If you're sure you'd like company, I could go home and get my own. It really would hit the spot, I can tell you." She smiled and wished she had a beer for him.

"I'm positive I'd like company if you don't mind going home for beer."

"Don't mind at all. I'll be back in a minute or two," he said, delighted for the company.

She went into the house after he left and put a bag of popcorn into the microwave. She had to admit she was happy to have company, too. The microwave beeped, and the corn was popped. She found a bowl large enough for the whole bag and grabbed some napkins. She was just going out the door when Pete came around the side of the house.

"Oh, geez, you didn't have to go and do that, Karina," he said. She noticed he had two beers in his hand.

"Oh, Pete, it's nothing. Here give me one of those. I'll put it in the fridge for you," she said, with a grin.

They settled into the old wooden chairs and sipped their drinks. The bowl of popcorn was between them.

"So, Karina," Pete began, "what are you going to do with the place? Do you know yet?" he asked, helping himself to some popcorn.

"I don't know. If I sell it, I'll make a fortune, but I really don't know."

"Ah, that's a tough one, for sure. Wouldn't you like having a place to come in the summer, though?" he asked.

"Yes, that sounds great, but I don't know if I would have time. My job keeps me pretty busy."

"Oh, yes. The *job*," he said, taking a sip of his beer.

"What do you mean, Pete? You say job, as if it were the enemy."

"It can be, Karina. We live in a world that is driven by success, and in this day and age, success is equated with nothing more than the accumulation of large sums of money. How stupid that is, really," he said, sadly.

"You know, Pete, I've been giving that very thing a lot of thought since I've been here," she said, seriously.

"How do you mean?" he asked.

"Well, I sell real estate, and I was awarded sales-person-of-the-month a while ago. I was absolutely blown away with the feeling I got!" She couldn't believe she was telling him this. "I really think I neglected my family. Can you believe that?"

They talked for a long time, more than they had ever talked in all the years they had known one another. He was a wise old man. Then they sat awhile and didn't talk at all, and they were comfortable doing that, too.

"Pete, I have to ask you something," Karin said, breaking the silence. "I can't remember if you had a wife or not. I just remember you alone."

"Oh, I had a wife, Karina, a long time ago. We had a little son, too, and one day she said she had to leave, just like that. She said 'Pete, I've found someone who makes me feel whole. You never did that, so I'm leaving. And Joey can stay with you.' I couldn't believe it; I thought I would die. Then in time I wanted to kill her. My boy and I came up here and lived in that old shack. You probably don't remember it," he said, but she did. "Then in time we were able to tear it down and build us a decent house. My son is a good boy. Well, he's not a boy anymore. He's a man."

"I'm so sorry, Pete," she said.

"So was I," he said, with a grunt. "But I got over it."

"I don't know how women can do that. How can they leave their own kids? Didn't you do anything?"

"What could I have done? I just took care of my boy and did the best I could," he replied.

She shook her head. He seemed like such a nice man and Grandma and Grandpa had always liked him. How could his wife have done such a thing?

She looked at her glass; it was empty.

"My glass is empty, Pete. Is your beer gone?" she asked.

"By golly it is. Good thing I brought two," he said, feeling so comfortable with this grandchild of his old friends.

"Let's go into the house and get a refill," she said, getting out of her chair and slapping her arm. "Maybe we should stay in. The mosquitos are starting to bite."

The phone rang just as they got to the door. She had completely forgotten about calling home.

"Okay if I use your bathroom, Karina?" Pete asked, as she reached for the phone.

"Sure, Pete," she said, then, "Hello."

"Hi," Brian said. "You sound happy. What are you doing?"

"I'm visiting with an old friend," she said. "How are you?"

"I'm fine. What old friend?" he wondered.

"Do you remember meeting Pete at Grandma's funeral?" she asked.

"Not really," he answered.

"Well, he's eighty-six years old and was a friend of my grandparents, and he's come to visit tonight."

"My God, Karin. One night a man brings you supper and the next night you have another man visiting you! What has happened to you ?" he asked, teasing her.

"Isn't it something?" she said, laughing. "He's so nice, Brian. I've known him for many years but never talked to him as much as I have tonight. He was very good to Grandma after Grandpa died. How's Kaitlin?" she asked.

"She's fine, but I think she's missing you."

Oh, good, she thought and said, "Really?"

"Really," he said. "Only four more days and you'll be home, right?"

"Only three and a half more," she said. Suddenly that seemed so far away.

"Well, I'll talk to you tomorrow then. I love you."

"Love you, too, bye," she said.

Pete came out of the bathroom.

"If it's getting late for you, I'll just go home, Karina," he said.

"It's only nine o'clock, Pete. Let's sit in here and finish the popcorn. That was my husband on the phone. You met him at the funeral. Do you remember?" she asked.

"Sure I do. I remember how your grandma used to brag about him, too. She liked him a lot." The curtains blew softly, and they sat quietly a bit, sharing the popcorn and enjoying the night air without the bugs.

"Pete, what ever happened to Elvira?" Karin asked. "I completely lost track of her."

"Oh, that was sad. She wasn't well and couldn't live here alone anymore, so she went to a nursing home. It was the one thing she dreaded. She talked about it often. 'Pete,' she'd say, 'I'd rather drop dead in the middle of the kitchen than end up in a nursing home.' She was a funny old gal," he said. "And as nice as she could be."

"I remember her well," Karin said. "She used to come over on Saturday nights to play cards." She smiled, remembering some pretty hot canasta games "We had a lot of fun. I don't remember, though, did she have any kids?" she asked.

"Yes, one daughter. She's the one who placed her in the home. It's not far from where she lives, I guess. I have Elvira's address and every once in a while I send her a card and she writes back. We were neighbors for a long time, and if I were younger, I would take a day and drive over to see her, but it's too far for me now." he said.

"But writing to her is awfully nice, Pete. Is she

with it? I mean she's not senile, is she?"

"Oh, I think she's sharp as a tack, but the arthritis got so bad she couldn't get along without help. She writes to me, but I'm certain she's not doing the writing. Someone else does the actual writing, but it's her thoughts, I can tell." They sat silent, remembering their old friend. Karin could picture in her mind that old black Buick disappearing around the bend in the road.

"Whatever happened to your cousin, Sonny? Was that his name? I remember him," Pete asked.

"Yes, Sonny. Do you really remember him? Gosh, that was a long time ago. He and his mother came up almost every other weekend. We had so much fun then. Hey, were you the one who told him there was a fifty-year-old muskie living in the bay? We spent a whole day trying to catch him," she said, laughing.

"Oh, geez, I probably did. Ah, that was mean. I shouldn't have done that," he said, laughing, too. "He was a nice kid, that Sonny. Every now and then he would show up at our place for some reason or another, usually just to talk. Yes, he was a nice boy. I liked him a lot."

"He's married now and has three kids. I don't see him very much anymore," she said, suddenly feeling sad, remembering the fun times they had here.

"Holy cow!" Pete exclaimed. "It's after ten o'clock. I should be getting home," he said, getting up from his chair. "I didn't mean to stay this long, Karina. I'm sorry."

"Oh, please don't be sorry, Pete. It's not late. I

really enjoyed your company, and I'm so glad you stopped. Maybe I'll see you again before I leave on Sunday. I'll know by then if I'm keeping the house or not, I hope."

"You give that some serious thought, Karina. I know it's worth a lot of money, but think how nice it is here. You could come up with your little family and enjoy the peace. I'd sure like to see you now and then," he said, as he headed to the front door. It had grown very dark. She turned on the outside lights and walked beside him to the road where they stopped for a moment.

"Thanks so much for coming over tonight, Pete. I really had a good time," she said.

"Me, too. I'll be talking to you," he said over his shoulder and waved. She could hear him whistling as he walked.

She was smiling as she locked up the house and got ready for bed. She couldn't remember the last time she had sat and visited with someone for two hours. It had been very pleasant. She got into bed with Grandma's journal and propped herself up on pillows. She had marked the page where she stopped reading, so she could find it easily. Her mother was now two years old and Grandma wrote.

*I am teaching this little rascal about the potty. She does pretty well, but then gets so busy playing that she wets herself. Then she cries because she didn't go on the potty like Mommy does. I don't think it will be long before she has better control, as she catches on quickly. I do put a diaper on her at night still. This will be great, no more diapers to wash and fold. Carl helps with potty training in the evening and Mary Beth loves when he praises her.*

Karin took off her glasses and rubbed her eyes. She had never washed a diaper in her life. Grandma probably had a ringer washer then, too, and no dryer, of course. She slipped her glasses on and read some more.

*I think I'm pregnant again! I hope and pray that I am. Mary Beth would love a brother or sister. Someone to play with every day.*

A few entries later the pregnancy was confirmed. Both Grandma and Grandpa were thrilled, as they had been with Mary Beth. Karin put down the book, removed her glasses, and wished once more that she'd had more kids. She stared at the ceiling and wondered why she hadn't.

"Well, it's too late now," she mumbled. She knew lots of women did have children at forty; it was possible, but not for her. She reached over and turned out the light, then cuddled down in her grandma's bed. She'd been gone from home almost one week.

Karin saw no sunrise Thursday morning. Oh, it happened alright, but she was fast asleep.

# ~9~

She woke at seven-thirty. Stretching, she smiled and looked at the clock. She had slept like a baby. This life was starting to agree with her. She rolled out of bed and pulled up the shades to another sunny day. She opened the window and felt the fresh air fill the room. She *felt* sunny today. She was calm, rested, at ease with life and pretty sure she would keep this house. She wasn't sure what she would do today though, and after a quick shower, she went down to the lake with a mug of coffee. The lake was calm and a cool breeze blew gently over her.

Sitting on the bench she contemplated keeping the house. Of course she would discuss it with her husband when she got home. She thought about some things they could do inside to make it look more like their home: some different furniture, maybe new curtains . . . new dishes.

She went back to the house and had a little breakfast, then stood in the big room looking around the place with a second mug of coffee. Maybe she would box up the dishes and linens, take them to the Good-

will and go shopping for new things. Then when
they all came up for a weekend, it would feel more
like home. Still not sure if that was what she wanted,
she realized that she had been awfully happy these
past few days and didn't think it was because she
was alone. She thought it was this place. She really
did love it and wished she could have some plants;
they did so much for a home. Grandma had many,
but they all had died.

Then it dawned on her that she didn't have to
decide what to do with the house this week. They
could keep it awhile and see how they liked it. With
that settled she decided that she would like new towels and sheets, for sure. Thinking some more about
that, she planned to go into town and do some shopping. She would definitely look at dishes, too.
Grandma's were old and not very pretty. She would
get boxes in town and pack up the old things. Feeling energized by the thought of making this her
home and having something to do all day, she began
making a list. Going through the cupboards and the
linen closet, she wrote down the things she would
need to buy. She would get dishes and a set of glass-
ware, too. The pots and pans were relatively new
and in good condition. She would keep them. Tomorrow she would take the old things to the Goodwill
in town.

With her list in hand, she got her purse and went
out to the garage. She would be back a little after
noon. She was sure she could finish today, buying
it all anyway. Then she had the rest of the week to
do it all. It would be fun; she hadn't done anything
this domestic in years. Phyllis, her cleaning lady,

took care of the house. She couldn't remember how that had happened. She used to love fussing around the house, rearranging furniture, getting something new, just making it nice for herself and her family. Somewhere along the line she had changed.

She drove with the windows down. It felt wonderful! At the department store in town, she found sheets for both the beds in the house. White with small pink flowers for Katlain and white with navy stripes for her and Brian. She would keep the bedspreads that were on the beds for now. She found some towels that were thick and fluffy. She carried her purchases out to the car and locked them in the trunk; then she went back in the store to look at dishes. There were lots of patterns to choose from; it was hard to decide. She picked a set that was white with tiny yellow flowers around the rim. It was plain and pretty, a service for four. She thought that would be enough. The glasses she found would go well with the dishes, and they were on sale.

From there she went to the grocery store where she bought a roasted chicken that would last her for days. She still had lots of salad greens and some rolls, so she was all set. Passing the floral department in the grocery store, she looked at the plants. They looked so pretty and healthy, that she stopped and picked out a philodendron. It would look great on the table in the big room for the rest of her stay and then she would bring it home. Her home could use a new plant or two. The ones she had weren't looking too well. She asked the bag boy at the checkout if she could have some boxes and he went in

back and brought out several of different sizes. She
thanked him and put them in a cart and pushed it
out to her car. She stopped at a drive-in and got a
hamburger for lunch. She really did feel sunny
today.

Back at the house, with everything unloaded from
the car and put in the big room, she wasn't sure
where to start. She thought the sheets should be
washed before putting them on the bed, so she
unwrapped them and put them in the washer. Then
she stripped the beds so they would be ready for
the clean sheets. She wouldn't hang the sheets out
this time, even though they smelled so nice when
she did. It would be quicker to put them in the
dryer. With that started, she began putting
Grandma's towels into one of the boxes. She left a
few of the nicest ones in the closet, because extra
towels were always needed at a lake house.

When the sheets were washed, she put them into
the dryer and the new towels in the washer.

"My goodness, Karin, you are rather efficient
after all," she said. It had been quite some time
since she had done this sort of thing and she was
moving right along. The kitchen cupboards were
next. She hoped they didn't need new liner, because
she hadn't thought to buy any.

"I should have known," she sighed, inspecting the
cupboard shelves. It looked as though Grandma had
just put down new liner. She was a very good house-
keeper. Karin knew that.

She started to feel hungry and checked the time.
It was nearly six o'clock. She couldn't believe it!
The time had gone so fast and she was done. Every-

thing new was clean and put away, and Grandma's things were all boxed up and ready to go. She opened the cupboards one more time; they looked nice and neat. She had accomplished much this afternoon and now it was time to eat.

She poured a glass of wine and sat down in the big room. She had rearranged the furniture in here, and it looked much cozier. The plant that she bought looked nice on the table, and the whole room was beginning to look like her home. Closing her eyes she put her head back, remembering the roasted chicken she had bought at the store and was happy not to have to cook anything.

After supper she went down to the pier. Her stay here was almost over. She didn't want to leave, but she missed her family. She definitely would plan a weekend here with them soon. Sitting on the bench, she watched the lake; several small boats dotted the water. It was so quiet tonight, and she was sleepy. She closed her eyes and pictured her mother in her red and white striped two piece swimsuit teaching her how to swim. She was ten years old and learned to swim not far out from the pier. She was scared to death, but her mother had been patient.

~~~

"Okay, Karina, I want you to float on your belly," she had said.

"I'll sink and drown. I know I will!," she cried.

"How can you sink if I have my hand under you all the time?"

"But will you?" she cried.

"Did I say I would?" her mother asked, with her hands on her hips.

"Yes, Mother, but I'm afraid!"

"Well, that's good in a way, Karina. You never want to get too brave in or around water; that way you'll always be cautious and that's important. Come now and lie down on my hand."

She had done as she was told and even put her face in the water.

"You're doing great, Karina," her mother said over and over. They spent the afternoon in the water that day.

"My goodness, look at my back. I look like a lobster!" her mother said.

"I'll put on some of that cream Grandma has for you, Mom, okay?" Karina offered.

~~~

She smiled remembering how carefully she had applied the cream to her mother's sunburned shoulders and that her mother had not taken her hand from under her until she asked her to. She had learned to swim in a few weeks that first summer and completely lost her fear of the water, but she always remained cautious. She sat listening to the crickets chirping for a few minutes, then feeling tired, she went up to the house. She was in bed early tonight with Grandma's journal. In two and a half days she would be back home. She was still undecided about the house. In a perfect world, the three of them would live here happily ever after.

"In a perfect world," she murmured, opening the book at the marked page and continuing to read about her grandmother's young life.

*I have had morning sickness this time; maybe it's*

*a boy! But maybe it's a beautiful girl like my Mary Beth and that will be fine too. I was never sick before.*

Karin dozed off, and when she woke, it was three in the morning. The journal lay in her lap. She wanted to read more, but was too tired, so she turned out the light and fell back to sleep. Waking early in the morning, she was surprised that she felt as rested as she did. She pulled up the shades and opened the window nearest the bed, then propped herself up on the pillows to read more from Grandma's journal.

*I am so depressed; today would have been little Carl's eighth birthday. I am huge with child, but still miss my first son. Nothing in life prepares us for the loss of a child. I think of women who lose a child after many years and cannot imagine it. My baby was only eighteen months old, and I miss him still. I am so grateful for what I have. I'm not complaining, really I'm not. I'm looking forward to delivering a healthy baby very soon.*

*Mary Beth has been potty trained for some time now and is turning into a well-behaved little girl. She knows we will have a baby here soon and knows where it is, now. She is fascinated that a baby is in Mommy's tummy and tells Daddy about it almost every night at story time.*

Karin smiled; her Grandma wrote about her feelings so well. She thought about starting a journal herself, and how nice it would be for Kaitlin to read about her life after she was gone. She swung her legs off the bed and walked barefoot into the kitchen to make coffee. It was Friday - not much time left for her here. Today she would drop off her grandma's things at the Goodwill. That was all that she had planned; then she could just lie around and read.

"Sounds good," she said, aloud. After showering and dressing, she put the boxes into the car. She poured a mug of coffee and went down to the lake. It had become a ritual for her, having coffee on the pier every morning. There were several sailboats on the water this morning. They always had such a calming effect on her. She finished her coffee and went up the wooden stairs. Something scurried in front of her foot. It was a chipmunk. She would stop and buy some peanuts in the shell while she was in town.

She remembered how Grandpa used to sit on these steps and feed them from his hand. She was always a little leery of letting them eat from her hand, thinking they may bite her.

Back in the house, she rinsed out her mug and went out to the garage. She wanted to get back early from town. She was eager to read more of the journals.

She drove to the Goodwill first and then stopped in at the engraver. She was assured the stone would be done the following week. She stopped at the cemetery, too, not knowing when she would be back.

"I'm going to keep your house, Grandma," she said, quietly to the mound of dirt, not sure when she had made up her mind. "I have to talk to Brian first, of course, but I'm sure he'll feel the same. I love it so much, and I promise I'll take good care of it. Thank you, Grandma. I love you," she said, and left.

She stopped at the little store and bought some peanuts for the chipmunks.

"Oh, it's you again. Nice to see you. How long will you be staying?" the gum-chewing girl asked.

"I'll only be here until Sunday, but I have a feeling you'll be seeing me again," she said, smiling. The girl stopped chewing and stared with her mouth open, waiting for an explanation.

"Thank you," Karin said, accepting her change from the girl.

"You have a nice day now," the girl said, chomping on her gum again.

"You, too," she said waving, and went out to her car.

She was back home, as she referred to the house now, before noon and had nothing to do until she left for home on Sunday. This pleased her. She had accomplished more than she expected she would during her stay here, and much of it was inside her head. She felt much more settled now. Before making her lunch, she went out and scattered some peanuts on the steps where she had seen the chipmunk earlier.

She took her sandwich and milk out to the front porch where it was cool. Situating herself in Grandma's rocker, she opened the journal where she had left off and read while she ate.

# ~10~

*It is eight o'clock in the evening and I think I'm going into labor. Mary Beth is asleep and Carl has called his mother to alert her of the situation. She will come and stay with Mary Beth while I'm gone.*

*It is one o'clock in the morning and the pains, when they come, are intense. Carl has gone to pick up his mother. I don't know what I would do without her. She has become a mother to me since my own died.*

*I look at my sweet Mary Beth while she sleeps; she is beautiful. We have talked about this event often, so she will not be alarmed to wake and find me gone. I have written a note that my mother-in-law will read to her when she wakes. I hope they return soon, as I am more than ready to go.*

There were no more entries for ten days or so. Karin knew that new mothers stayed in the hospital much longer in those days.

*I'm supposed to be taking a nap, but I want to write something. Carl's mother is here helping me and has told me to lie down and rest, which I will do in a minute. We had a baby girl and named her Mildred Louise. I love the name Mildred and Louise is for my mother. She is every bit as beguiling as her sister. We are all fine.*

Days later.

*I am alone now with the girls. I'm rested and strong, thanks to my mother-in-law. She helped me so. Carl is a great help when he comes home from work and Mary Beth helps, too. She is an excellent runner. Just when I get settled with the baby at my breast, I need something and she can get it for me. She is also learning to answer the phone, which usually rings when I am with the baby. She shows no signs of jealously as we always speak of this child as her baby. Carl calls the baby Millie Lou. It's sweet, but I don't think I want the name to stick.*

"And I thought Karina was bad!" Karin exclaimed, continuing to read, intrigued by all she was learning about her grandmother.

Later in the journal.

*I have had a miscarriage! I didn't even know I was pregnant. Carl had to take me to the doctor as I was bleeding so. Millie is only one year old, but another baby would have been welcome.*

Karin read on about her aunt's young life.

*Millie is learning about the potty. Mary Beth is surprisingly helpful and her sister is doing well.*

*Carl has built a playhouse in the back yard for the girls and they love it. Most days they have their lunch out there as they hate to leave it. It is so much fun to watch them play. They are very good mothers to their dolls.*

Then Grandma wrote.

*I have miscarried again and almost bled to death this time. Dr. O'Donald said I shouldn't become pregnant again. We don't know what is wrong, but he said I would be taking a great risk if it should happen again. I feel awful, I wanted so to have a boy for Carl. I tell him this and he says, "Oh, Lizzie Beth. I have you and two beautiful daughters. What more could a man want?" I don't know what I would do without him.*

By now Karin had read through four journals, and there were a few more in the dresser drawer. She took her plate and glass into the house and rinsed them in the sink. It was only two o'clock. She could read for hours more. She went back out on the porch, sat in the rocker and opened the journal that she had been reading.

*Mary Beth started kindergarten yesterday and Millie is lost without her. We walk her to school after breakfast. Millie rides in the stroller. I wish she went in the afternoon, as Millie would be napping and not miss her so. However it gives the two of us a chance to be alone. I'm sure she will adjust.*

*Mary Beth loves school and has announced that she wants to become a teacher, when she is big. She draws a picture for us almost every day and most of the time we know what it is suppose to be. She has met several girls with whom she likes to play. We will have them over after school sometime to play in the playhouse.*

Karin read until three o'clock. The time had passed so quickly. Her whole body was beginning to feel numb though, so she went inside and put the book on the table. "I need to walk," she muttered, and went back outside. She walked to the road and turned right. This would take her past Pete's house and around the bend to the main road, then eventually back to her house. It was a pleasant walk and took about thirty minutes.

Passing Pete's place, she saw him on the porch. She couldn't go by without talking to him.

"Hi, Pete," she called to him. He looked up from the paper he was reading and waved to her.

"Hi, there, Karina! What are you up to?" he asked. She followed the path from the road to his house.

"Oh, not much," she said, sitting down on the steps. I've been sitting reading Grandma's journals, and I need to exercise a little. I just thought I'd follow the road around."

"That's a great walk. Do it often myself," he said. "It's the right distance, just far enough. Don't let me keep you then. Go on with your walk."

"Yes, I should. I've been sitting too long. Oh, by the way, Pete, I'm keeping the house. I don't know how I ever thought I could sell it."

"Oh, great! I'm real glad to hear that. Maybe I'll see you now and again. I'd like that," he said, smiling at her.

"I feel it's the right thing to do, and I think Grandma would want me to keep it," she said, getting to her feet. "Well, if I don't see you again before I leave, Pete, I'll be back. I want to bring my family here for a weekend, soon." They said good-bye and wished each other well.

This was such a nice place to walk. The trees formed an archway over the blacktop road so it was shady and cool. It had been gravel, when she was a kid all those years ago. She and Clare walked here often, picking black raspberries as big as their thumbs and eating most of them before they got back to the cottage. She had wonderful memories of her summers here.

Back at the house after her walk, she opened a can of soda and took it and the journal down to the pier. She was absolutely fascinated with her grandmother's writing, never realizing she had documented so much of her life. Karin made a promise to herself that she would start a journal when she got back home. It was never too late to start.

She sat on the bench and waved to a family passing by in their boat. Opening the book she began to read. She was well into the fifth journal now, and it still held her interest. She read along for a few minutes, sipping her drink, when she came to an entry that shocked her.

*I have found a letter from a woman amongst some of Carl's papers. I was looking for an address of an old friend of ours. I am seething with anger, to say the very least. This is not my imagination, the letter says it all. How can this be happening? This man, <u>my man</u>! I feel so stupid! Why didn't I know?*

Karin was indeed shocked. Her grandpa? One of the nicest men she had ever known? And Grandma, what was wrong with her? She wondered why the hell hadn't she thrown him out. She continued reading.

*I approached Carl about the letter last night after the girls were in bed. He denied nothing, but said it had ended. I asked him why, he said he didn't know. He cried, and he hasn't done that since little Carl died. I feel empty and betrayed. I don't want him near me.*

It continued days later.

*We talk about this problem often. I'm grateful that he will. I don't know how I could bear this if I couldn't talk. I hope someday I will feel the way I did about him before I knew this, but right now that seems impossible.*

Karin took off her glasses and rubbed her eyes, her faith in humanity nearly destroyed. If Grandpa could have done this, then she was sure anyone could. She was getting hungry, but simply could not stop reading.

*I am so confused, I don't know what to do. Carl has slept on the sofa since I learned of his indiscretion. It seemed okay at first, but I don't know how that can bridge the gap between us. I am not eager for much more than to lie in his arms. I do need that. I wish my mother were alive now, but then I know I would never tell her this if she was.*

*Carl is a good man I know. I can't understand how this happened. And were there no signs? Am I really that stupid? I don't think that I should ruin my life and my daughters' lives because he did a foolish thing. I have told him this. We will all lose if I ask him to leave. I think he just lost track of himself and made a mistake. I will help him get back on track, but he will have to be patient with me, as this has been a blow! If it should ever happen again, he will have to find his own way back without the girls and me. I somehow think it won't. I love him more than he knows, or is capable of loving. We women are so different from men. It's just the way of things, I suppose.*

Karin couldn't believe it yet. Her soda was gone, and she was really hungry now. She climbed the wooden steps with a heavy heart. She wondered what she would do if the same thing happened to her. How had Grandma done it? No one would have known. They loved each other dearly, and their devotion to one another had always been obvious. She had always been impressed with her grandparents and the love they shared. Maybe today people are much too inclined to give up the minute something isn't just as they think it should be. Most of the people she knew were on their second marriage, at least.

She looked through the fridge and found something to eat. She wished Brian were here now. She missed him. She wondered what she would do if he did something like that. How would she know? Grandma hadn't. But she knew she couldn't watch him, or worse, have him watched. It was just so unsettling. She ate at the table in the big room and continued to read.

*The girls think I may be sick, as I am not my usual self. I have told them that I think I have a touch of the flu. I am working hard at this marriage. I, for one, believe it is worth it. Carl has been so loving and kind and has apologized at least one hundred times. I told him that was enough. We are getting back to normal. I am so glad. He says he worries that maybe I will do the same thing to get back at him. I tell him that is almost as offensive to me as what he did.*

*Isn't it a wonder, really, that men and women stay together, being so very different? I think it's all part of a plan, where one is weak, the other is strong and never the same person all the time. I can remember many times when he has supported me. I know now that I love him a lot and I am grateful for him. But we both know that we will not go through this again.*

Karin rinsed her dishes in the sink, still stunned. "Who would have known?" she whispered, and thought that when we're young we think we know much more than older people and assume they have never experienced some of the adversities that we have. These journals were surely enlightening. Grandma was a wise woman it seemed, but no martyr. She just understood her husband and valued her family, and she made it clear that it would not happen again, at least not to her. Karin wondered if her own mother had known of this affair, and rather hoped that she hadn't.

# ~11~

It was seven o'clock in the evening and she had read enough for one day. She poured a glass of wine and took it down to the lake. The day after tomorrow she would go home. She wondered if she should go tomorrow, as she was really lonesome. They hadn't even talked today. She would call when she went back up to the house. The lake was so still tonight, and only a few boats were out. It was peaceful. She sipped her wine and watched the water, still thinking about her grandparents. According to the journal, it had taken a very long time for Grandma to work through what had happened to her, probably longer than Grandpa was aware.

Then she heard something up in the yard. Someone was calling her. She stood up and shielded her eyes. There was a man standing at the top of the stairs. She couldn't make out who it was, because the sun was so intense in the western sky. "Oh, my God!" she exclaimed when she recognized him. "Brian, is that you?" she said, scrambling up the stairs. It struck her that if he was here, something must have happened to Kaitlin.

"Oh, nooo . . . . Why are you here?" she asked, almost shouting at him when she reached the yard.

"Why am I *here?*" he asked, puzzled, holding her at arms length.

"Has something happened to Kaitlin?" she asked.

"No, Kaitlin's fine. I just got tired of being alone," he said, taking her into his arms.

"Oh, I didn't mean to yell at you. I just got scared for a minute. I'm so glad you're here! I was just thinking about going home tomorrow. I've missed you," she said, kissing him.

"Well, I thought maybe we could stay here until Sunday as you planned, except we'll be together. Kaitlin is next door with Cindy. She's babysitting for them tomorrow night, so they said she could stay over tonight and tomorrow. Is that okay with you?" he asked.

"It's more than okay with me. I've done a lot of thinking since I've been here, and I want to tell you all about it. Oh, I'm so glad you came! It's a great surprise. Would you like a glass of wine?" she asked. He would have preferred scotch, neat, but said he would love a glass of wine.

"Have you had dinner?" she asked when they were in the house.

"Well, sort of. Not really," he said.

"Should we get a pizza? Let's, I didn't eat much either. I'm still hungry. I'll call, and then we can go pick it up. We'll get a bottle of scotch, too," she said, knowing what he liked.

"Sure, it's fine with me. Hey, the place looks different somehow. What have you done?" he asked, wandering through the big room. She was on the phone, ordering pizza with all his favorite toppings.

"Fifteen minutes? Thank you," she said into the phone.

"Do you like it? I have made a few changes. I'll show you all of that tomorrow. I'm so very glad you're here," she said, cuddling up to him. He hugged her tight to him and said how much he had missed her. They stayed just like that for a few minutes, both realizing how lonely they had been. She wondered, now, how she could have thought he was distant.

"This is the nicest thing you could have done, Brian. I'm so happy you're here," she said. "Let's go; it will take five minutes to get there. "Who's buying?"

"You are," he said. "I'm driving." And so off they went to the pizza parlor, happy to be together again.

She was very quiet in the car.

"Is something wrong?" he asked. "You're awfully quiet." She was still thinking about what she had read in the journal, but wasn't sure she wanted to tell him.

"Nothing's wrong, but I've been reading Grandma's journals most of the day. I think I was still in the past when you surprised me," she explained.

"Should you be reading that stuff? Isn't a journal private?" he asked, turning into the parking lot.

"So, here we are at the business district," he said, laughing. He always called it that: The gas station, where you could also get bait, the store with the gum-chewing clerk, a tavern, and a pizza place.

"What more do civilized people need?" he added.

"Nothing," she said. She loved it and was used to it after all the summers she had spent here. To her it was a step back in time. "Do you want some scotch? Go get a bottle while I get the pizza," she said as she headed toward the door of the pizza parlor.

Back in the car she thought about what he had said about the journals being private. It had never occurred to her not to read them.

"Why would someone write all that and leave it to be found if they didn't want anyone to read it, the journals, I mean," she asked.

"Well, I suppose you're right. Why would she? It just seems so personal to me," he said.

"I'm going to start one when I get home. It's interesting to read about my mother and Aunt Millie when they were little kids, and other things, too," she added.

When they got back to the house, she took two new plates out of the cupboard. He noticed.

"Don't you have any paper plates?" he asked. "There isn't a dishwasher here if I remember correctly," he said, going to use the bathroom. Ignoring him, she put place mats on the table in the big room and then the new plates. She put ice in the new glasses and added water. Then she poured two fingers of scotch into a short glass for him and some wine for herself. She lit a candle and put it next to the plant on the table. The setting looked inviting. She slid the pizza onto the serving plate that came with the dishes so everything was ready when he came out of the bathroom.

"Wow!" he said, smiling. "This is really nice." He gave her a quick kiss and pulled out the chair for her.

"Thank you, Dear," she said. "I bought these new dishes just yesterday. Do you like them?"

"Yeah, they're nice," he said, helping himself to a piece of pizza. "This is great pizza. I haven't had any this good in a long time."

"I've decided to keep this house, Brian. What do you think? Is it a good idea?"

"Well, why wouldn't you? It's a beautiful place. I never thought you would sell it. Did you actually consider it?" he asked, surprised.

She couldn't figure out how everything could be so simple for other people. She had spent days pondering this, and he just knew what to do.

"Do you have any idea what this place is worth, Brian? There's one hundred feet of lake front out there," she said, sounding like a realtor.

"So, how important is that?" he asked, confused now. "If you sell it, we can't come up here. Did I miss something?"

"Well, we're always so busy working, that I didn't know if we would ever find the time."

"Wait a minute," he said, quietly. "Who's always busy? How many times have I asked you to go somewhere, and you're too busy. If it's a weekend, you're showing a house; if it's a week day, you're busy at the office." She thought about what he said, took another piece of pizza and ate the whole thing before saying anything. He wasn't the one who had been distant at all; it had been her.

"That's true, isn't it?" she said, softly.

"Hey, I'm not complaining - just stating a fact," he said, not wanting to anger her.

"The last piece is yours. I'm stuffed," she said. He was surprised, she rarely ate until she was full. "Want another drink?" she asked.

"I would. Thanks," he said, taking the last piece of pizza. She got up and went into the kitchen, thinking about what he had said. She had been so focused on her work. She came back to the table with the bottle, poured some into his glass and sat down.

"Since I've been here, I've been thinking a lot about that very thing," she told him.

"What do you mean?"

"Well, how my job has become the most important thing in my life, and I have you and Kaitlin. I'm really sorry. I think I've neglected you both," she said, truly meaning it.

"Oh, now do I look neglected?" he asked, laughing.

"I'm serious, Brian. I've given it a lot of thought, and some things are going to have to change," she said, standing and picking up their plates. He took his scotch and followed her into the kitchen.

"What has to change? Aren't you happy?" he asked, then added, "I suppose we have to wash the dishes now."

"No, we're not washing the dishes, and yes, I'm happy, but I just want to change some things. Let's go down to the lake. Do you want another drink?" she asked, knowing he would say no. He was a two drink man, never more, seldom less. "No, I'm fine," he said, rinsing his glass.

She led the way down the wooden stairs to the pier where they sat close to each other on the bench.

"Isn't it beautiful here, Brian? I love it so much. I hope we can come often. It's like another world, but only three and a half hours away." They sat in silence for a while, watching the water.

"The water is like life; always moving, always changing," he said, pulling her closer to him.

"Well, that's very profound, my dear," she said, smiling and turning to kiss him.

"Ah, yes. That's me," he said, laughing and returning her kiss.

"Look at all the stars; there must be billions!" she said, sounding like a kid. She was so content to sit with him here. "I'm so happy you came. Did I tell you that?"

"Only about ten times, I think."

"When did you decide to drive up?" she asked.

"Yesterday."

"I'm so glad."

"Well, actually we ran out of stuff to eat, and you know how I hate going to the grocery store," he teased.

"You're awful," she said.

"Are you tired?" he asked.

"Yeah, are you?"

"Yes. I was busy today trying to get everything done so I could leave early. If I had thought about it before, I would have taken off the whole day."

"Lets go up then," she said, standing and taking his hand. "I have brand new sheets on the bed."

"My, aren't you the little homemaker?" They went up the stairs together, his hand cupping her bottom.

Inside the house, they locked the doors and got ready for bed. She was waiting for him when he came out of the shower. She pulled the covers back on his side of the bed, and he climbed in. It was then that they realized how very much they had missed each other.

~~~

She woke before he did the next morning and watched him sleep. She loved doing this. He looked so funny. His mouth was open a bit, and he snored softly. His eyes were moving rapidly and she thought he must be dreaming. She crept carefully out of bed so as not to wake him and padded barefoot to the kitchen. She started the coffee, and then opened the windows in the big room. The breeze blew the curtains softly and filled the room with fresh lake air.

There were eggs in the fridge, but no bacon. Hmmm, she thought. Cheese - there was some of that. She would make cheese omelets and toast. She set the table in the big room and poured juice into her new glasses. She was glad that she had done some shopping. It made this house seem more like her own.

"It is your house, silly," she whispered. He was leaning on the doorjamb watching her.

"When did you start talking to yourself, Dear?" he asked.

She jumped. "My God, you scared me!" she said. "I thought you were still sleeping." She went to him and put her arms around him, thrilled that he was here with her.

"Want some coffee?" she asked.

"Yes, I'll get it, though. You do whatever it is you're doing," he said. "What exactly are you doing?"

"I'm making cheese omelets for our breakfast, and we'll have toast with jam. How's that sound?" she asked, busy whisking the eggs.

"Sounds great, but do I have time for a shower?"

"No. And if you wait until we've eaten, I'll shower with you."

"Such a deal," he said, smiling. "Breakfast and a shower with a pretty lady."

"Yeah, right. Like I don't know what I look like in the morning," she said, laughing.

After breakfast and a long shower together, they were dressed and ready for the day.

"I want to call Kaitlin before we do anything," she said, as she put the last dish away in the cupboard. She hung up the dish towel and went to the phone, amazed that she didn't mind washing dishes that much. They had always had a dishwasher, and sometimes she hated to even load it. She dialed her neighbor's number and waited.

"Cindy, it's Karin," she said. "Fine, how are you? Good, is my daughter there?" After a moment Kaitlin came to the phone.

"Hello."

"Hi, Sweetheart. How are you doing?" she hadn't talked to her since leaving for the lake over a week ago.

"Hi, Mom. I'm fine. Did Daddy tell you I'm babysitting? I love it, and I've saved most of my money so far . . ." she rambled on and on. Karin was smiling as she listened.

"Hey, time out! I miss you, Katie."

"Oh, I'm sorry, Mom, I didn't mean to talk so fast. I miss you, too. Are you still coming home tomorrow?" she asked.

"Yes, we'll be home tomorrow, but we're all coming up here for a weekend very soon. Would you like that? Maybe Sharon can come with us sometime," she added. Kaitlin and Sharon had been friends for years, after meeting in the first grade.

"That would be great! Oh, I have to go, Mom. Cindy wants me to go to the store with her and help get the groceries. I'll see you tomorrow then, right?"

"Right. See you tomorrow," she said, then added, "Love you," but her daughter had already hung up the phone. Karin missed her, but Kaitlin sounded busy and happy. She hadn't been surprised that they would be coming to the lake house either. Perhaps she had been the only one who had considered selling it.

"We're going to have to buy a boat," Brian said, coming into the kitchen. "No sense having a house on a lake without one. I'd like to go out there this morning," he announced.

"And do what?" she asked. "You sure don't like to fish."

"No, but I'd like to take a ride around and see how big this lake really is, now that I'm a home owner here." She smiled at the way he said that.

"I could ask Pete if we could borrow his. I'm sure he wouldn't mind," she said.

"Ah, I don't know about that," he said, looking out at the lake. "It's been a long time since I've been out. I think I'd rather wait until I have my own boat."

"Okay, now we have all day. What would you like to do?" she asked. "Let's take some coffee down to the lake and decide. That's what I've been doing every morning." She poured mugs of hot coffee, and they made their way down to the pier. It was another beautiful summer day, and many boats were out on the water.

"See that one out there?" he said, pointing. "That's what I want."

She squinted her eyes against the sun and asked. "That one? It's a cabin cruiser. Don't you think that's a little extravagant?"

"Yes, Dear. I'm only kidding. I just want a boat with an inboard motor."

"Have you ever considered a sailboat?" she asked. "They look so serene. I watch them in the evening. There are always two or three out then."

"I think they can be tricky though," he said. "But I suppose we could learn," he added. They finished their coffee and decided to take a drive.

# ~12~

In the car, with Brian at the wheel, they drove around the lake.

"This is such a beautiful drive," she said, happy to be watching the scenery instead of the road. There were acres of wooded areas and lofty evergreens that seemed to go on forever. There were deer-crossing signs along the way as this was their home, and without notice, they often walked out onto the road. The window was open, and her shoulder length hair was blowing softly. He turned to her to say something and stopped himself. She looked so pretty with little or no makeup, much more like her old self. He noticed that her brow was furrowed; that meant she was pondering something, he knew. He looked back at the road and felt her looking at him. He turned to her once again.

"What?" he asked.

"Nothing. I didn't say anything," she said.

"I know, but you're thinking about something. What is it?" She turned in her seat to face him.

"Do you ever wish we had more kids, Brian?" she asked, seriously.

"Oh, I don't know. I'm pretty happy with what I have. Why?"

"I just wondered."

"You're not thinking of having one now, are you?" he asked, hoping like hell she wasn't.

"No, I'm too old. It would be too hard to start over, and I don't think it would be fair to any of us now," she said. He was relieved to hear that. He worked with a man who was older than he and had just had a new baby. He had two older kids and his wife wanted another to keep them young. He said it was a nightmare. It had disrupted his whole family and made him feel anything but young.

"I've done so much thinking since I've been here, and I wish I had another child. Did you know that my grandmother had two miscarriages?" she asked.

"Now how would I know that?" he asked, patiently.

"Well, I guess you wouldn't. I didn't, but it was in her journals. I told you they had a little boy who died though, didn't I?"

"I think I remember you telling me that, yes," he said.

"Can you imagine how horrible that would be? If something happened to Kaitlin, I mean?"

He wondered why she was doing this - thinking about all this depressing stuff? They rode in silence for awhile looking at the homes along the lake until he spoke again.

"Are you unhappy? You sound as though you regret your life," he said.

"No, not at all. I just don't think I've been paying much attention to what's really important and I'm sorry about that," she said. "Let's stop here for a minute; this is directly across from our house and at night you can see our pier light. That's what Grandpa said anyway. We used to come here for ice cream."

"I've got the binoculars in the glove box. Let's have a look," he said. She took the glasses out and looked across the lake.

"I can see it! I see our pier. I guess we didn't have these things when we were kids," she said, handing him the binoculars.

"Do you want some ice cream as long as we're here?" he asked.

"No. Let's have lunch first, okay?"

"Okay," he said, putting the car in gear.

She was frowning again.

"Now what is it? You're doing it again," he said.

"Doing what?" she asked.

"Frowning."

"Oh, sorry. I was thinking about Grandma. She had a lot of sadness in her life and, I never knew. Her mother died when she was real young, not long after she and Grandpa married. Then they lost their baby, then the miscarriages then . . . I don't know, it's just sad," she said, not sure if she would mention Grandpa's affair or not.

"I think we should be happy for what we have," he stated. "You can't miss what you haven't had. We only had one child. So we haven't lost anything. Let's be happy we have her."

"I am, for sure, and I miss her," she said. "About a mile or so farther there's a place to eat. Want to stop? It's not fancy, but the food is good."

And so they stopped, three quarters of the way

around the lake, to have some lunch. They ordered fish and chips. It was the speciality of the house.

"I can't remember when I had fish and chips, can you?" she asked.

"Been a long time for sure," he said. "It's very good."

"Let's go to the Shore Club tonight, shall we? They have the best steaks around. I think we'll need reservations, though," she said.

"Do you have something to wear?" he asked. "I only have casual clothes with me."

"Oh, it's not that fancy. They just don't allow shorts. You brought your tan slacks didn't you?"

"Yes," he said.

"That will be fine. I brought a sun dress. I could wear that."

"Is it that little black backless one?" he asked.

"Yes, it's very cool."

"And very sexy," he said. The waitress came to their table and asked if they would be having dessert.

"I don't think so, thank you," he said, picking up the tab.

"Are you ready to go?" he asked.

"Yes, but I think I'll use the bathroom first." He watched her walk away from the table and wondered what was going on with her. She was ruminating on something, he knew that, and he also knew that she would eventually tell him. She always did. She seemed different somehow, too, more like she was when they were younger. He rather liked it. He paid the bill and waited for her by the door. He smiled when he saw her walking toward him. She looked so . . . cute. That was it, cute. She was suntanned and looked rested.

"You ready?" she asked, flashing a big smile.

"Yep," he answered, holding the door for her.

"Now what?" she said, fumbling in her purse for sunglasses.

"Well, we could keep going around the lake," he offered. "Or go to the Shore Club and see if we need reservations for tonight, or both."

"Let's go to the restaurant first. That way we'll be sure to get in later."

"I'm not sure I know how to get there," he said, backing out of the parking space.

"We have to go back a bit and get on the highway. Then turn left," she told him.

They made reservations for seven o'clock that evening. They had the rest of the afternoon to themselves. This was rare for them to be free and alone together on a weekend, and it felt good.

"We should do this more often," he said.

She turned and watched him drive. He was so handsome, she thought, and so masculine, not macho. She hated that in a man. She was sure he didn't know how strong he was in so many ways. Yet he could be so gentle, too. There was no pretense about this man. He simply was . . . . She had done one thing right for sure. She had chosen him.

"Okay, what are you looking at?" he asked, not taking his eyes off the road.

"You, my love, and may I say your peripheral vision is excellent." He put his hand on her knee and squeezed.

"What's up with you anyway? You're acting rather strangely. Do you know it?" he asked.

"Yes, I know. There's no one stranger than me. I thought you knew that."

"Let's go home and take a swim. Maybe I'll hold your head under water awhile and see if that helps," he said, teasing.

"You're terrible," she said, laughing.

They arrived back at the house and changed into their swimsuits.

"I'm surprised you remembered to bring your suit," she said.

"Well, I like to be prepared for anything," he said, grabbing a towel from the linen closet. "Let's go."

The water felt cold just for a moment or two, then totally refreshing.

"This feels great," he said, floating on his back. "Another thing we have to get for the house is an alarm system."

"I never thought of that. Yes, we should," she said. The house had been empty while Grandma was in the hospital and after she died, but they couldn't leave it that way forever. They agreed that she would call and make the arrangements. After an hour or so of swimming and lying in the sun, she announced that she was going up to the house.

"I'm going to shower and wash the seaweed smell out of my hair. Then I'm going to take a nap. Nude!" she shouted, as she picked up her towel and ran up the wooden stairs. He scrambled to his feet, grabbed his towel and was right behind her.

~~~

Later, he woke and moved just enough so he could see the clock, careful not to wake her. They had fallen asleep together like two spoons in a drawer; they seemed to fit together perfectly this way.

"I'm awake," she said, then moved away from him a bit and rolled over onto her back. She smiled at him and stretched.

"We should definitely do this more often," she whispered. Then curled up on her side with her face against his chest inhaling his fragrance.

"You smell good," she murmured.

"How long do you think it's been since we did that in the middle of the afternoon?" he asked.

"Too long," was all she said. They stayed like that for a while, so content together. He was thinking about how much he loved making love to her. She was wondering what to do with her hair. She threw back the sheet and sat on the edge of the bed, tousling her hair with both hands.

"Should I wear my hair up tonight?" she asked.

"If you want. It would be cool, but I like it either way. Are you wearing that little black dress?" he wondered.

"I was, but is it *too* little? You always call it my little dress." It was rather short and backless. Perfect for summer.

"No, it's not too little. I love it. It's a little less dress than what you usually wear, I guess," he said.

"Well, of course it is, silly. It's a sun dress," she said, with that *don't you know anything* tone.

~~~

They arrived at the restaurant fifteen minutes early and decided to have a drink at the bar while they waited. It was nearly full already, but they found one empty stool. She climbed up on it, and he stood behind her. Country western music played softly in the background. At eight o'clock that would change to live local musicians, who played loudly. He ordered for them both and put money on the bar. When their drinks came, she turned in her chair a bit, so they could talk.

"Are you hungry?" she asked. "We ate lunch early."

"I'm starved," he said. "What should we get?"

"The steaks are great. I think I'll have that," she said, sipping her wine.

They sat quietly for a few minutes watching the other people at the bar. He had his hand on her bare back and was stroking her neck with his thumb.

"Parker, Parker table for two," the hostess said.

"Yes, that's us," Brian said, leaving a tip on the bar. He followed Karin, who was following the hostess to a table by the window. When they were seated, she handed them both a menu and told them that prime-rib was the special this evening and the soup was French onion.

"Enjoy your dinner," she said, with a smile.

"Thank you," they said, together. They looked over the menu and decided on the New York strip. She smiled at him and took a sip of wine.

"I'm really glad you came," she said.

"I'm glad I did too," he said, reaching for her hand.

"Another drink for you two?" the waitress asked, as she poured water into their glasses.

"Not for me," Brian said.

"I'll have another glass of wine, please," she said.

The music in the restaurant was not the same as

what they had heard in the bar. It was softer and more contemporary. They were eating their salads and commenting on how good they tasted, the rolls, too. They were crisp on the outside and soft and warm inside.

"I wish I could make rolls like this," she said, breaking a piece off one and buttering it.

"Have you ever tried?" he asked.

She thought a minute and shook her head. "No, I don't think I have."

"Well, maybe you should," he offered.

Grandma always did and she had watched her plenty of times. Oh, she baked cookies and cakes and muffins, but had never tried breads. It sounded like fun to her now and remembering how wonderful the house had smelled made her even more determined to try.

"I think I'll do that this fall, when it's not so hot," she said.

When their salad plates were cleared, they sat quietly and watched the lake. The view was beautiful and the night perfect. What would she have been doing now had he not come up to be with her? She enjoyed the few moments between dinner courses and took the opportunity to tell him what she had read in Grandma's journal, not sure just when she had decided to reveal it.

He took a sip of water and stared at her.

"You're serious? Now see that's what I mean about those things being private. I don't think you should read anymore," he stated.

"Are you defending Grandpa?" she asked, curiously.

114

"No, not at all. I'm really surprised to tell you the truth," he said.

"It makes me feel bad," she said. "Like he wasn't who I thought he was and I don't like that. It worries me some, too. I wonder if there are any men who can be trusted." There, she said it, that's what was really bothering her.

He just watched her; he could tell that it upset her. So that's what all her seriousness had been about. He knew she would tell him sometime. Their dinners were brought to them and the usual questions asked.

"No, I don't think we need a thing, thank you," he answered. They ate in silence for a few minutes.

"Isn't this great?" she asked. "I told you the steaks were good here."

"Best I've had in a long time," he said.

"I suppose I shouldn't be upset - it's none of my business," she said, picking up the conversation where they had left it.

"Well, it's no one's business but theirs, but I can see why it would make you feel bad. I know how much you loved him," he said.

"It really does, and I hate feeling this way about him," she said again.

He took a bite of steak and thought, as he chewed. "If your grandma could forgive him, don't you think you should be able to?" he asked. "Forgiving him doesn't necessarily mean you condone what he did, you know," he told her. She smiled and shook her head.

"What? What's funny?" he asked.

"Nothing. You're just so wise sometimes," she

answered.

"Sometimes?" he asked.

"Yes, Dear, just sometimes." She was quiet for a few minutes, eating and sipping her wine.

"I don't know what I would do if you did something like that," she said, softly.

He was watching her and she was serious. "I don't think you have to worry about that, Karin," he said, quietly.

"That's what Grandma thought, and that's why she was so blown away."

He felt sad for her and smiled. "I'll tell you what, if some drop dead gorgeous woman ever comes on to me, I'll simply tell her that I'll have to ask you about it first. Okay?"

She smiled her love for him. "I'm sorry. I don't doubt you, really. I was just so shocked when I read that."

"As you should be," he said. "But don't let it cloud the good memories you have; that would be a mistake."

"I won't," she whispered. "Let's have dessert tonight," she said, getting back to the present. They both had coffee and shared a sinfully rich chocolate dessert.

After dinner they walked down the stone path to the lake and looked back at the restaurant, high on a hill. With a light in every window, it was beautiful against the darkening sky. There were many boats docked tonight. Most of the people who lived on the lake took their boats to the restaurant instead of their cars.

"We'll do that next summer, Karin," he said. "We

have all winter to decide what we want."

"Let's walk out on the pier and look at them closer," she said. There were some beautiful ones, for sure. Two of them looked like small yachts.

"Those two must belong to the people who live in the mansions we passed today," he said, softly, knowing they couldn't have one that fancy, but loving them nonetheless.

After walking around for a bit, they went back to the car and drove with the windows down and the music loud. She reached over to turn it down a little.

"I wish we could ride home together tomorrow," she said.

"So do I," he replied. "Next time we will and every time after that."

"When should we leave?" she asked.

"I'd like to be home early in the afternoon," he answered.

"Me, too. We should leave by ten or ten-thirty," she said, not really wanting to go now that he was here.

It was almost ten o'clock when he pulled the car up to the garage. A light shone in the big room. It was on a timer, and it welcomed them into the house.

"I think I'll leave that light on the timer when we go home," she said.

"Good idea. When the alarm system is installed, I'm sure you'll feel better," he said.

"I will, I know, but I may still have a light going on and off, it makes it look more lived in. Are you going to bed, or watching the news?" she asked.

"I think I'll watch it for awhile. I don't know

why I'm so tired," he said.

"It's all the good fresh air here," she told him.

She went into the bathroom to wash her face and get ready for bed. She opened the bed and turned on the light beside it. He came into the room as she was opening one of the windows.

"No good news, as usual. I'm going to bed," he said.

"Me, too. Did you turn off everything?" she asked. She knew the doors were locked. She had done that, when they came in.

"Yes, Dear, I did." They got into bed and kissed good night.

"Thank you again for coming. I was really starting to miss you," she said.

"Me, too," he said, kissing her again. She reached up and turned out the light. Within five minutes his breathing became deep and even. He was asleep. She envied that. He could always go right to sleep, no matter what. She tried to get comfortable and make her mind go blank, but couldn't. She turned over several times and gave up. Why she had coffee with dessert she didn't know. It always kept her awake. She couldn't just lie here, and she couldn't keep flopping around, she would surely wake him. Sitting up carefully, she noticed that it was eleven o'clock. She picked up the journal she had been reading and crept out of the room closing the door behind her.

# ~13~

She turned on the light in the big room and settled herself on the couch with her legs curled beneath her. She quickly found her place in the book and began reading what Grandma had written.

*The girls think they are too big to play in the playhouse any longer. They would like to sell it and use the money for new bicycles. We told them we would think about it. Mary Beth, now thirteen, thinks she's too old for many things; such as a specified bedtime during the school year and much more. Millie would play in the little house, I know, but she tries to be just like her big sister. They are quite a pair, these two girls of ours.*

*It has been settled, after much thought and discussion. The playhouse stays. When we are sure they no longer want it, Carl will store garden tools in it. I think he's proud of it. He built it from scratch and it looks nice in the yard. They will get new bicycles for Christmas.*

Karin took off her glasses and rubbed her eyes. She was still wide awake. She continued reading, stopping long enough to get a glass of water.

*Mary Beth has been invited to a school dance. The boy is in her history class. I can't believe it! She's growing up so fast.*

Karin read through her mother's high school years and on to her marriage. The entries were less often now that Grandma's children had grown. They had their own lives, but events and holidays were always noted.

*Mary Beth is expecting her first child. We will be grandparents! Carl is nearly as excited as he was with our own.*

~~~

*We have a new granddaughter! She is absolutely beautiful - just like her mother. I will stay with Mary Beth for a few days to help. She has named this child Karola. I have not heard this name before, but I said nothing.*

So, Karin thought, Grandma thought the names were odd, too. She had never said a word, even when she and her sister dropped the "a." Still not sleepy, she read on, skimming over parts that didn't hold her interest.

*Mary Beth has told us that she is again pregnant. We are delighted! We love this grandparent thing. Karola will be four when the baby comes. I secretly hope it's a boy.*

"Ah," Karin whispered, hoping she hadn't been a disappointment to anyone.

*Another girl. As beautiful as the first! We are so*

*happy and Karola loves her so much. It reminds me of my own two daughters when they were small. This child has been named Karina. Pronounced Ka-ree-na, Mary Beth has told us. I will stay with them a day or two and then have Karola here for a bit so Mary Beth doesn't have them both until she's stronger.*

Karin looked at the clock. It was twenty minutes to two. "I will read until two o'clock and then go to bed," she said to herself, feeling like maybe she could sleep now. She had read up to Grandpa's funeral.

*I can't believe he's gone and I don't know what I will do now that I'm alone. There were always things to do with Carl. There was no warning; that's the hardest part. He just left without a word. The funeral service was nice, I'm told. I don't think I heard much. I wish I could go with him. I'm eighty years old. What am I going to do now? A big part of me died with him. I feel as though half of me is missing.*

There was a water spot on that page. Karin knew it was Grandma's tears. She read through the weeks and months after Grandpa's death. It had been so hard for Grandma. She was grateful that she had managed to spend as much time with her as she did. Every visit from the kids, friends and neighbors had been noted. It had helped her get on with things. Then, years later . . .

*One of the worst things has happened. My Mary Beth has cancer. Why not me? They tell me nothing can be done. How can that be in this day and age? I'm so mad I could scream! I wish Carl were here. I need him so much.*

Karin's mother's illness and death were documented in detail, much like her childhood. Grandma felt so helpless, all she could do was write about it. She spent as much time as she could with her oldest daughter as she died, her heart aching all the while.

*We buried Mary Beth today. I feel hollow, as though there is nothing left in me, not even one more tear. Karola and Karina have been so good to me and strong through it all. I know this is hard for them. They are both too young to be without their mother, even though they are grown women with children of their own. It should have been me. I should have been the one in the casket, not my Mary Beth. Kaitlin sat next to me. She is such a sweet child.*

Karin closed the book and put it on the table. She could sleep now. She felt relaxed and tired. She turned out the light and went back to bed. Brian hadn't moved. She kissed him softly, turned on her side and drifted off to sleep, certain now that she should start a journal of her own.

~~~

She was down by the pier, checking the fishing lines that Sonny had in the water.

He did this nearly every day, but never caught a thing. She was on her knees, pulling up the lines from the water, with nothing left on them but the hooks. The worms, now long gone, had been a juicy snack for a fish or two. Sonny was calling to her from the top of the stairs.

"Karin! Karin!" Why did he call her Karin? He never had before.

"Karin!" he said, again. "Aren't you getting up?"

Getting up where, what? She opened her eyes. She was in bed, and she had been dreaming.

"Are you getting up today?" Brian asked, laughing at her.

"What time is it?" she asked.

"Eight forty-five," he answered.

"What are you laughing at?" she asked, squinting at the clock. It really was that late.

"Oh, you just wake up funny," he said.

"I was dreaming. I thought you were Sonny," she said, throwing back the covers and sitting up in bed. He was all dressed and looked ready to go.

"What time did you get up?" she asked.

"About an hour ago. Want some coffee?"

"Love some," she said. "I couldn't sleep, so I got up and read some more. I think I went to bed at two."

"Well, it's no wonder you're tired. Want to sleep some more? You're still on vacation, you know," he said.

"Oh, no. I've got lots to do. Don't let me forget

my new plant, Brian. It's on the table. It will die if I forget it." He went out to the kitchen to get her coffee.

"I put the plant on the counter in the kitchen. You can't miss it," he said, returning to the bedroom and handing her a mug of fresh coffee.

"Thank you. Did you eat yet?" she asked.

"No, I was waiting for you. What do you want?"

"Not much. There's some cereal. Is that okay?

"Fine with me. Want some toast too?" he asked.

"Sure, I'll be right there." She went into the bathroom with her coffee. She could sleep some more for sure, but wouldn't. She was eager to get home, and she had two stops to make first. She wanted to go to the cemetery once more, and then into town to buy a journal. She was serious about starting one.

They needed only to pack their clothes and empty the fridge of anything that would spoil before their return. This was their second home now, and she loved it. She set three timers in different parts of the house and closed all the shades. Soon she would be back for the installation of the alarm system. She hadn't even left yet and was already thinking about when she would be back. She knew she had made the right decision now.

Brian was out putting his bag into his car. They were ready to go. Her new plant was in a cardboard box on the front seat of her car.

"Well, I'm ready, are you?" he asked, coming in through the breezeway from the garage. "I put your stuff in your car. Do you have anything else to take home?"

"No, I'm all set, but I'm going to stop at the cemetery and at the bookstore in town, so if you get home before me, don't worry," she said, gathering her purse and the stack of Grandma's journals. Looking around to make sure everything was the way it should be, she went to kiss him. "I'll see you at home. Thanks for this weekend."

"Drive carefully now," he said and returned her kiss. He was so happy he'd come, he had really missed her.

She backed out of the garage and got out of the car to close the overhead door, determined to get an automatic opener as soon as possible.

"Sorry, Grandpa," she muttered, remembering how he felt about that. She drove to the cemetery first and left the car running. She wasn't staying long. Walking towards the grave, she saw the date of Grandma's death was engraved already. It looked nice and matched the other engraving almost perfectly.

"Good-bye, Grandma, and thank you again for your wonderful house. I love it so much. Brian came up, and we had such a nice time. He loves it, too."

She brushed away a tear and pressed her fingertips to her lips. Bending down, she touched Grandma's stone, then did the same to Grandpa's.

"I'll be back soon," she whispered, got into her car and drove away.

She drove into town and then thought of Pete. She had wanted to say good-bye to him, too. She arrived at the bookstore and went straight to the card section and selected a suitable one for him. She would drop it the mail box at the curb in front of the store when she left. She found the counter where the journals were displayed and looked at many of them until she saw one that she liked. It was beige in color with pictures of leaves on the front. There were no dates inside. She liked that because she wasn't sure she would write every day. She would write the date each time she made an entry, just like Grandma had done. She paid for her purchases and wrote a short note to Pete before leaving the store. She dropped it in the mailbox at the curb and got into her car. She had taken care of everything here. Now she would concentrate on getting home to her family and her job, not a small task.

# ~14~

Brian's car was in the garage when she arrived home, and the door was up. She was suddenly so happy to be back here. Just then Kaitlin came out of the front door, excited about something.

"Hi, Mom," she said, running towards her. Karin threw her arms around her, nearly lifting her off the ground.

"Hey, Katie. I'm so glad to see you! How are you?" she asked, stepping back to look at her. She was such a pretty girl. She looked a lot like Brian, but had her mother's hair and eyes.

"Mom, guess what?" she said.

Karin thought a minute and said, "I give up. What?"

"You know the people next door to Cindy?" she asked, helping Karin take things out of her car.

"Well, I don't really *know* them, but I know who they are. Why?"

"Their cat had kittens, and you know what? They're free to good homes," Kaitlin told her mother, watching her face for a reaction.

Karin was taking a bag out of the trunk and

127

peered out from behind the lid at her daughter. "And? What does that have to do with us?"

"I thought maybe we could have one. I could take care of it, you know."

"Oh, I don't know about that. We don't know anything about cats."

"Please, Mom, we could learn. They're so cute. You'll have to see them."

Karin closed the trunk and walked around the side of the car.

"Would you get the plant for me, Honey? Oh, the presents in that bag are for you and Dad.

"Sure. A present? Thanks, Mom. Um, could you just think about it, Mom? The kitten I mean. Please?"

"Of course I'll think about it. We'll have to ask Dad, too, you know," she warned. What she didn't know was that Kaitlin had already talked to her dad, and he said it would be okay if her mother agreed.

"Of course, we have to ask him," she said, smiling smugly.

The remainder of Sunday flew by. There wasn't much to do in the house, as Kaitlin and Brian had kept it neat. Karin appreciated that and told her daughter so. Kaitlin loved the white sweater her mother had bought for her, and it fit perfectly. Brian wore his new golf shirt all the rest of the day, even though Karin thought it should have been washed before wearing.

~~~

Karin and Kaitlin inspected the new kittens and one was chosen. They were too young to leave their mother yet, but would be ready in about two weeks. Kaitlin was excited and wished she didn't have to wait. The neighbor assured her that she could visit the kitten whenever she wanted.

~~~

Monday morning was busy at Carson Realty and Karin felt out of sync. It would take awhile to get back in the swing of things. She hadn't given this place a moment's thought while she was at the lake house. She was going through her messages and mail, when her boss told her he wanted her to take a ride out to the old Wentworth house.

"The old lady wants to sell. She can't manage it alone anymore," he said.

"Can I finish this first?" Karin asked.

"Oh, sure. Go, whenever you want. I told her we would try to get out today."

"Okay, Brad, I'll get to it sometime today, for sure," she told him. After an hour or so of catching up on things, she picked up her purse and left her office.

"Lillie, I'm going out to Mrs. Wentworth's. It shouldn't take more than an hour. Tell Brad when he comes back, will you?" she said, passing the receptionist's desk on the way out.

"Will do. See you later," Lillie responded.

The drive to the house was pleasant - the sun was shining, and the radio was playing. She had no trouble finding it and was happy to be out of the office. She turned into the driveway that led to the house; it was long and winding. She noticed that here and there along the drive, small low lights were placed. "This must look lovely at night," she murmured. She parked her car in the horseshoe drive near the house and went up to the door. She heard the chimes inside, when she pushed the doorbell. In a moment the door was opened by Mrs. Wentworth herself.

"Mrs. Wentworth, I'm Karin Parker from Carson Realty," she said, offering the woman her hand.

"Please come in," the older woman said, taking her hand. "Call me Julia."

"Thank you, Julia."

The foyer was large and beautiful. The chandelier above was from another time.

"Oh, Mrs. Wentworth, I mean, Julia, this is so beautiful," Karin said, taking in the beauty of this house.

"Thank you. Come, I'll show you around." It was like stepping back in time. Some of the furnishings were as old as the house and in excellent condition.

"The Historical Society has offered to take the furniture. I wish they would buy the house as well and preserve it," Julia said.

"Have you asked them about it?" Karin wondered, thinking it was a great idea.

"I have spent the last nine months pursuing that with no luck. They simply do not have the funding. I can't donate the house, as I have to think of my children," she said. "I'm giving them the furniture and that will be placed in the museum," she added.

They went from room to room, and Karin was awed by the place. A period house in good condition on three acres of land was worth a great deal of money. She was surprised at how blase she felt. Two weeks ago she would have been mentally calculating the commission on the sale. Today she was enjoying this woman and her very beautiful home.

The tour of the house ended where it began, in the foyer.

"I do so wish you could stay for tea," Julia said.

"I wish I could, too," Karin said, really meaning it. "But you see I've been gone from work for six days and I have a lot of catching up to do."

"Oh, I understand. We will be talking soon, though, right?" the older woman asked.

"Yes, we will. It will be a pleasure showing this house, Julia. It truly is spectacular," Karin said and went out to the porch. She turned and took Julia's hand in her own.

"It was very nice meeting you, Julia. Thank you for showing me your home. I love it."

"The pleasure was mine. I'll be waiting for your call," Julia said. "Good-by, now."

~~~

Karin was home a whole week before she found time to start her journal. She wrote the month, day and year at the top of the page and the day of the week under that. Then she began recording her life as her grandmother had done all those years ago.

*I have been through a renaissance of sorts. I spent nine days at the lake house I inherited; seven of those days I was alone. Brian surprised me and came up on Friday. We had a great time together. We must do it more often. I've done some heavy duty thinking, and I'm going to spend much more time learning how to live. I want my daughter to learn the difference between a good work ethic, which I feel is vital, and greed. I have talked with my boss about going to part-time and will know*

*next week if he approves.*
*I will try hard to keep this journal up to date, like*
*Grandma did.*

The following Sunday, Karin cooked a special dinner for her family and set the table in the dining
room. Kaitlin saw it and was puzzled.

"Mom, are we having company? What's going on?"
Karin was busy in the kitchen.

"No, Honey, we're not having company. Would
you pour some water in those glasses for me, please?"
she asked.

"You mean all this is for *us* ?" her daughter asked,
filling the glasses.

"Yes, just for us," Karin replied, feeling rather
proud. It did look nice. Weekend meals were usually "grab what you want when you want it," but
today it would be different.

"I think it's cool, Mom. I like it." Brian was out
on the driveway washing the car. He would be surprised, too.

The roasted chicken was delicious, and the conversation was interesting. After dinner they all
pitched in to clean up so it didn't seem like work
at all. Karin suggested a journal to Kaitlin, explain-
ing how she had found her great grandmother's at
the lake and how much she enjoyed reading them.

"Great Grandma really wrote her whole life in
books?"

"Well, not everything. A person couldn't do that,
but special events and things. I've started one of
my own and thought you might like to start one,
too. I'll pick one up for you next time I go shop-

ping, if you want me to. That kitten is almost ready to be adopted, that would be something to write about. Think about it.

~~~

In bed that night, Karin was propped up with pillows against the headboard reading her grandma's final journal. Her own was close by.

*I am not feeling well, but can't even describe it. Perhaps it's old age. Who would have thought I would live to be <u>ninety</u>? I'm more than ready to be with Carl and my other kids. I wonder if anyone at all will be interested in reading about my life. If not, I believe it helped me sort through things better, being able to see it in writing.*

This journal, the one Karin had found on the night stand beside her grandmother's bed, was only half filled. Then Grandma died. Her last entry was . . .

*I feel worse today. I have a headache, too. Quite unusual for me. If I'm not feeling better in a day or two, I'll have to call someone to take me to the doctor. I hope it just goes away.*

But it didn't just go away. She had a stroke that very night and went to the hospital for one week. Karin had been called early the next morning and had taken off work to be with her grandmother. That seemed so long ago now, but it had only been a little over two months. So much had happened since then.

She put down the journal and picked up her own, wishing her grandma knew how very much she loved reading about her life. Then Karin wrote . . .

*Tomorrow is a work day. Somehow it doesn't excite me as much as it once did. I look forward to part-time. I have so many ideas for this family and our two homes. The new family member will join us this week. I hear cats are easy pets to care for. I'm hoping so, as I know little about them.*

Then she turned out the light and lay on her side, carefully backing into Brian. She liked to be touching him, when she slept. She thought about when he had kissed her good-night. He told her that today had been great, and all she had done was cook a meal and serve it in the dining room. She went to sleep thinking how lucky she was to have him and their beautiful daughter.

The second week at work flew by, too. The Wentworth house was on the market and would be shown on Sunday. Karin would work the same until the end of the month, then go to three days a week and one open house a month. It sounded wonderful! She wasn't sure which days she would work, but hoped Brad would agree with Tuesday, Wednesday and Friday. That was what she wanted. It would give her so much time to do the little things that meant so much.

# ~15~

Kaitlin brought the kitten home in the middle of the week, after all the supplies needed for its care were purchased. A little basket with a liner for sleeping in, a litter box, a bowl and food for young kittens. Kaitlin wanted to keep the basket near her bed at night, but her parents decided that the kitten would be better off near its litter and food for the first few nights.

"I think she'll be okay in the kitchen," Karin told her daughter. "We can put a night light there for her, too." Kaitlin agreed it would be best, because if the kitten needed to use her litter box in the night, she may not be able to find it if it wasn't close by. She was relatively easy to care for and seemed very independent for something so tiny. The biggest dilemma seemed to be choosing a name for her. They were pretty sure it was a female, and Kaitlin wanted her to have a pretty name. Karin found a note pad on Kaitlin's desk as she was changing the sheets on her bed. Muffy, Molly, Muffin, Matty, Susie, Fluffy and so on. Cindy was written and crossed out. She must have thought it not appropriate to name the cat after the next-door neighbor. Karin agreed.

She smiled and picked up the pen, adding a few names to the list. She finished the bed and carried the sheets to the laundry room. It was a beautiful fall day; sunny, cool and the leaves were the vibrant colors of autumn. She opened the window. Someone was burning leaves, and they smelled wonderful. She loved having the laundry room on the first floor. It was so much more pleasant than having to go down to the basement.

They had lived in this house almost seven years. It was quite a find. Karin, being in the business, had seen it in the listing the first day it appeared. It looked perfect. She had talked to Brian about it and asked Brad if it would be possible for them to look at it before it was published. The three of them went to the house and looked it over thoroughly. It was just right for their needs, and Brian and Karin put in a bid that very day. They got the house, and were able to sell their own in no time at all. The whole transaction had gone so smoothly that she couldn't believe it. The house was eight years old and in good condition. A three bedroom ranch, with a family room and a fireplace. The laundry room was on the main floor. It had all the features that they had wanted so badly.

"We were meant to have this house," she had said. Kaitlin was six at the time and going into the first grade. The school was different, but she adjusted nicely. That was when Karin started working full time. The first year was part-time work as Kaitlin was in school only half days. She was ready for that part-time work again now, seven years later.

~~~

When Kaitlin came home from school, she went to her room, put her books on her desk and saw the names her mother had added to her list. Bitsy, Betsy, Annie, Patsy, and Mandy. She read the list thoughtfully, studying each name. She bent down and picked up the kitten, who had followed her into her room. Setting the ball of fur on her bed, she got down on her knees to look the cat in the eye.

"What do you look like? You are very pretty, and I want your name to fit you. Let me see, do you look like Annie? No, I don't think so. Mandy, Muffin? I wish you could tell me." The kitten purred in response. She loved her new home and the people in it. They could have called her anything; she wouldn't have cared. She was sort of a butterscotch color, with a white face and paws, and she had stripes on her tail. Brian said they were racing stripes, because she was very fast and loved to chase things. Kaitlin continued watching her new friend, and it hit her. Betsy. This kitten looked like a Betsy.

"Betsy, that's what we'll call you. Do you like it, my love?" She picked her up and went to find her mother.

"Mom! Mom, where are you?" she called.

"I'm in the kitchen," her mother answered.

"I've picked a name for her, Mom! I hope you like it."

"Which one did you pick?" she asked.

"Betsy. I'm going to name her Betsy. Do you like it?"

"Yes, I like it. Didn't I put that on your list?" her mother asked.

"Oh, yeah, I guess you did. Well, I think she looks like a Betsy. It's a pretty name for a pretty little girl."

"We *think* she's a girl Kaitlin. Oh, I called the vet this morning. We have an appointment this Saturday. I made it for Saturday, so you could go with us. She is your pet."

"Thanks, Mom. I want to go. I love her so much. I knew I wanted a pet, but I didn't know how much I would love her. I'm glad you and Dad let me have her," she said.

"I'm glad we did, too. She's a nice addition to our family. The weekend after that we're going to the lake house. We'll have to get a pet carrier for Betsy so she can go with us," Karin said.

"We can take her with us?" Kaitlin asked, surprised.

"Well, of course we can. We wouldn't leave you here alone, would we?" she said, scratching the kitten's ears. Karin was a bit surprised at how she felt about this tiny furry thing, too. She loved the way the cat curled up in her lap for a nap and how she purred when she was petted.

Everything was going well for the Parker family. Karin was working part-time, and Kaitlin was doing well in school. Brian was content to have his wife home more, and the kitten had taken over the house and the hearts of the people within.

*This cat is something else. She is very well-behaved and has used her litter box from day one without an accident. She sleeps in Kaitlin's bed at night now and anywhere she pleases during the day. We will*

*have her spayed when she is old enough. Brian says
we should have her declawed, too, but Kaitlin and
I aren't sure about that. It seems so cruel.*

~~~

*We took Betsy with us to the lake house, and she
is a good traveler. I feel better about the house now
as the alarm system has been installed. I hope we
can go again soon. It's beautiful there in the fall.*

The weather began to get cold as October turned
into November, but Karin's house was far from cold.
She had worked hard on her days off and painted
the kitchen, laundry room and half bath. She loved
being home more and had let Phyllis, her cleaning
lady, go a few weeks ago. Almost every day she was
home, she would light the fireplace around the time
she started dinner. It was a gas log so it wasn't any
trouble and it didn't make a mess. Why hadn't she
ever done this before? It was so inviting, and Brian
loved it when he came home. She would pour him
a scotch and insist he sit and look at the paper while
she finished dinner. He kidded and called her June
Cleaver, but she knew he enjoyed it.

Betsy was indeed a female and had been given
the necessary inoculations. She was a bit young for
spaying, but that would be done as soon as possible.
ble.
"The vet said it's best to do it before they come
into heat for the first time," Karin told Brian.
Kaitlin had spent some of her hard-earned babysitting money for an elaborate cat-condo for Betsy. It
was a climbing post with a sleeping box on top, and

it was all covered with carpet. She was happy to do it, but didn't know the best place for it.

"I don't think she wants to spend the day in my room, Mom, but I don't think you want it out where it shows," Kaitlin lamented.

"Why don't you put it in the family room by the window next to the fireplace? I've noticed that she likes to look out the window," Karin offered.

"You don't mind? Kaitlin asked. "I didn't think you would like it where it would show. It's kind of big."

She wouldn't have a few months ago. How odd, she had wanted the house perfect at all times. That's why she had Phyllis, but they had never really *lived* in the house.

"I think it will be fine there. It's a very nice place for Betsy to spend time, and I know you spent a lot of money for it. I think it will look okay."

That night before turning out the light . . .

*The Wentworth house sold this morning. An attorney has bought it and plans to have his office in the library. He and his wife have a great respect for the house and plan to keep it the way it is as much as possible. They have bought some of the furnishings that the Historical Society didn't want. We will share the commission of this sale as we all were part of the transaction. I am happy for Corrine. She's new and needs the money badly. She's divorced and has two little kids. She gets little help from her ex.*

Kaitlin had started a journal as well. She preferred a plain spiral notebook.

*This is my first journal. I am almost thirteen years old. My mom said I should write. She has started one and my great-grandma had one. I think that's where my mom got the idea in the first place. Anyway, I have a new kitten named Betsy. Well, she's not that new now. We've had her for six weeks or so. I bought her a climbing post so she won't have to have her claws pulled out. Me and Mom didn't like the idea much. I guess that's all for now.*

Karin wanted to paint the family room next. Brian insisted that they do it on the weekend, so he could help. When they bought the house, the paint had been fresh. That was seven years ago. They picked muted colors that went well with the carpet and blended with the colors of the furniture. It was an improvement for sure. She noticed everything now, to the extent that she had noticed nothing before. The result was fabulous! The house was renewed. It looked the way she felt.

She looked forward to the holidays more than she had in a long time. She had always been so busy and the holidays had sort of infringed on her busy schedule. Now she wondered how she could have been so, so . . . . She didn't even know what it was. She planned to have a celebration here and at the lake house sometime during the season. She would invite her sister, but didn't think she would come. She lived in another world and was busy most of the time. But she would try. She was toying with the idea of a small dinner party for the people at the real estate office. She would have to think about that.

She was doing well with her journal, writing at least three times a week, and happy that Kaitlin had begun writing, too. She hadn't read anything her daughter had written and wouldn't unless asked.

*I am so happy to be working only part-time. I have so many plans for the holiday season. I don't know how I was able to work full-time. I don't know how I did everything. Well, I guess I didn't, did I? This all seems so much more important to me now than working. I guess I have my grandma to thank for that. Had I not read her journals, I don't think I would have changed at all. Thank you, Grandma. My husband and daughter are happier, too, although I know neither of them would have asked me to give up my work. I'm glad it came from within me.*

~~~

*I have begun shopping for the holidays. I've nixed the idea of an office party here, as Brad and his wife are having something. I think I'll make a pan of lasagna and take it to work for lunch. Everyone would like that, I know. I'll bake some Christmas cookies, too - I'll have time this year.*

*Brian has been extra busy lately, so it helps that I am not. I regret not seeing this before, but I won't dwell on it. I regret deeply not having more children as well, but this is the last time it will be mentioned. I am so grateful for my family. Seeing how Kaitlin is with this kitten, I can't help but wonder how much fun a sibling would have been for her.*

*She has never mentioned it to us, therefore I assume she's missing nothing. Maybe she will have a few kids of her own someday, although I'm not ready for that yet!*

The house looked beautiful at the holiday season. Karin had outdone herself this year. There were decorations everywhere, but all in good taste. She had heard that cats sometimes climb up a Christmas tree, so she watched the kitten closely. Betsy was very interested in the tree and all its decorations, but had not touched it. She did, however, like to nap beneath it, so when it was time to put the presents under the tree, Karin left a small space for her to curl up and sleep.

~~~

Christmas was one week away and all the preparations were complete. Kaitlin was next door, babysitting for Cindy's kids and Karin and Brian were alone. They sat in front of the fireplace, with the tree lights and candles the only illumination.

"This is so nice," Brian said. "I don't remember a better holiday season, do you?" He pulled her closer to him and kissed the top of her head. Her hair smelled so good.

"I can't believe I'm finished with all my shopping. It's great! I feel so relaxed, and I did more this year than I have in a long time. I love being home more. I'm so glad I'm able to," she said, sipping her wine.

"Well, you never had to work, Karin. You know that," he said, quietly.

"Yes, I know, but that's the best part. When I

wanted to, I could. Now that I don't want to as much, I don't have to. I have you to thank for that, my dear." He just shrugged and took a sip of his drink.

"It's true, Brian. I'm very grateful for you. Do you know that?"

"Oh, geez, now don't get like that," he said, somewhat embarrassed.

"Don't get like what? I love you. You're a good husband and a wonderful father, and now I'm going get another glass of wine and go to bed. So there!" she said and marched off to the kitchen.

"Bed? It's only eight-thirty." Then he caught on and was in bed before she got there.

~~~

When Kaitlin got home from babysitting, they were sitting on the couch in their robes, as though they had spent the evening watching television.

"Oh, I didn't think you would still be up," she said, when she saw them sitting together.

"We were watching a movie," Karin said at the same time Brian said,

"We were watching the game." Karin poked him with her elbow and smiled. It had gone unnoticed by Kaitlin. She was watching as Betsy crawled sleepily out of the compartment at the top of her perch. She jumped to the floor, landing silently on all fours.

"I'm going to bed. Night, Mom. Night, Dad," she said, bending to kiss each of them on the cheek. "Come on, Betsy. Time for bed."

"Watching a movie?" Brian said, laughing as he pulled her down onto his lap. "Ready for bed?" he asked.

"Yes, I'm tired. Let's go." They turned out the lights and checked the doors before going down the hall to their room. Karin peeked in on Kaitlin. She was sitting up in bed with her spiral notebook. She tapped on her door.

"Night, again, Sweetheart," she said.

"Night, again," Kaitlin responded.

# ~16~

The holidays had been wonderful. They invited the next-door neighbors over for Christmas eve. Cindy was thrilled as she and her husband Don had no family here and were unable to go to either parents' this year. The two kids had a great time too. They loved being with Kaitlin and were fascinated with Betsy. After supper, they had gone out in the yard and made a snowman with the freshly fallen snow. The adults and Betsy watched from inside the house. Somehow it always seemed perfect, when it snowed on Christmas eve.

"Makes it much easier for Santa," Brian had announced.

On Christmas day, Karol and Ralph came for dinner and spent the night. Karin was excited as she didn't think they would, but at the last minute Karol had called and said they could make it. They were coming without the boys who were older now and wanted to stay at home. It had been fun for Karin and her sister, as they hadn't seen each other since Grandma's funeral.

"I wish you could stay longer, Karol," Karin had

said. But they couldn't. They were traveling half way across the country to visit relatives of Ralph.

"So do I, but duty calls," Karol said. She always called it her *duty* when they visited his family.

"Well, I can't tell you how happy I am that you came. Maybe we can meet up at the lake house sometime," she suggested.

"Or maybe you could fly out to New York, little sister. It's been years since you did that," Karol said, teasing. They hugged and kissed, thanked each other for the gifts and promised to write and call often.

During the week between Christmas and New Year's, they spent a few days at the lake house. That had been a wonderful time, too. They had Pete for dinner one night and talked until after midnight. He was an interesting old guy, and Brian got along well with him. He was crazy about Kaitlin and the cat, too. Karin had gotten a small tree with the lights on it to have at the lake. With that and a few candles in the big room, it set the mood for the season.

The New Year was heralded in by a blizzard. No one went anywhere that night. Karin and Brian invited Cindy and Don over and Kaitlin babysat for their kids. It was sort of a spur of the moment thing, so they pooled their resources and made dinner. Then they played bridge and welcomed in the new year together. It snowed for hours, and outside looked like a winter wonderland. The snow was beautiful, especially since they didn't have to go out in it. They had a quiet evening at home, and all four of them said how very nice it had been.

~~~

Carson Realty was slow after the first of the year, but that wasn't unusual, and Karin was used to it. She welcomed it in a way after all the activity of the past few weeks. Kaitlin was back to school and the house was back to normal. All the decorations were put away. It was a quieter time, almost like a lull in life.

Betsy was old enough to be spayed now and was taken to the vet early in the morning and spent the night there. Kaitlin missed her and didn't sleep well that night. Karin missed her, too, and picked her up the next day as soon as they would release her. They were all amazed at her recovery.

"How can she do that?" Karin exclaimed, as the cat jumped up on the couch. "I would be flat on my back if I had that done." Kaitlin seemed a little disappointed, she wanted to take care of the cat after the surgery.

"They aren't like us, Honey," Karin told her. "But you wouldn't want to see her in pain, would you?" Her daughter agreed. She wouldn't want to see her pet feel anything bad, ever.

~~~

On a cold night in February, Karin woke to a pounding sound. When she was fully awake and looked at the clock, she saw that it was twelve-twenty in the morning. Then she realized that the pounding noise was at the front door. She shook Brian awake and got up jamming her feet into her slippers and putting on her robe as she staggered down the hall. She flipped on the porch light and looked out. Cindy was standing on the porch with a look of horror on her face. Karin opened the door and pulled her neighbor inside.

"Cindy! What on earth has happened? My God, you're freezing!" By now Brian was at the door as well.

"Cindy, what is it?" he asked, puzzled.

"It's Don! The hospital just called. He's been in an accident, and he's in serious condition. What am I going to do?" She was crying now and Karin put her arms around her. She was so cold. She had stepped into some old shoes and run over in her pajamas. Brian went and pulled the throw off the couch, wrapped it around her and led her to a chair.

"Cindy, take a deep breath and tell us what they said," Karin said, handing her a tissue. Cindy gave her nose a good blow and pulled the blanket around her shoulders.

"They said he's in serious condition, and that I'd better come quickly," she said, wiping her eyes with the tissue. Just then Kaitlin came out of her room yawning.

"What's going on, Mom?" she asked.

"Honey, Don's been in an accident. Cindy has to go to the hospital. Put on some sweats and we'll go next door so the kids aren't alone, okay? Hurry, please," she added. "Cindy, I'll be right back." Karin ran to her room and pulled her nightgown over her head, put on a sweat shirt and pulled on a pair of jeans. She grabbed her shoes and was back to where Cindy and Brian were in less than a minute.

"Come on, Cindy. You have to get dressed. Brian will drive you to the hospital. Kaitlin and I will go stay with the kids. Hurry now."

Brian turned and went down the hall. He and Kaitlin were dressed at the same time. They went silently to the garage to get the car. Cindy was coming out of the house as they drove up her driveway. She looked a wreck, but she did have on clothes, shoes and her coat. Kaitlin got out of the car and held the door for her. She had no idea what to say, so she patted her on the arm.

"Tell your mother I'll call as soon as we know something, Kaitlin," Brian said, as she was closing the car door.

"I will, Dad," she said and waved them off into the night. Back in the house she looked questioningly at her mother.

"Dad says he'll call as soon as they know something."

"Good. Oh, I hope Don's okay," she said. She had an uneasy feeling about this, but didn't let on that she did to Kaitlin.

"Why don't you go lie down in Cindy's bed and go back to sleep. I'm sure she won't mind," she said, putting her arm around her daughter. Kaitlin did as she was told, and Karin checked on the two kids. They were sound asleep. She was grateful for that. She went into the family room and sat on the couch. She had a dreadful feeling in her gut, and wondered why they had told Cindy to come quickly. It didn't sound good. She sat in almost total darkness and thought about what just transpired in the last ten minutes - unable to believe it had happened. She was grateful that Brian had been home, and wondered what she would have done if she were alone. She got up and walked around the room. There was nothing she could do, and she hated that.

"Well, you are doing something," she told herself. "You're watching the kids." She picked up the remote, switched on the television and sat down again. She flipped through all the channels and muted the sound.

"Please, God, let him be okay," she whispered. She sat like that until the phone startled her. She picked it up after one ring.

"Hello."

"Karin, he's gone," Brian said, his voice was shaking.

"No! Oh, no. He can't be."

"He is," was all he said.

"Where is Cindy? Oh, Brian, how is she?" Karin was crying now.

"The nurse is talking to her about donating his organs; then she'll give her something to help her sleep," he answered.

"Oh, dear God, what will she do now?"

"Are the kids okay?" he asked.

"Oh, the kids . . . yes, they're asleep. How will she tell them? Oh, Brian this is so awful. Do they know what happened?"

"Someone hit him broadside, they said. He was alive when they got him to the hospital, but he was so bad, nothing they did helped. They put him on a ventilator until Cindy got here. I feel sick to my stomach. I'd better go. We'll be home as soon as possible. I'm afraid she's going to fall apart."

"I'll be waiting for you. I'm glad you're with her, Brian. You're strong," she said.

"Yeah, right. See you in a bit," he said, not feeling very strong at all at the moment.

"Talking to him about donating his organs? How revolting! How despicable can people be for God's sake?" she said to no one. She was shaking and pacing the floor, realizing that this is when those questions have to be asked. Thinking about that, she knew how difficult it must be for those people who do the asking. She wondered about what she would do in the same situation, but she couldn't even think straight now. "Poor Cindy and those kids. Why do these things happen?" she asked herself. She went into the bathroom and splashed her face with cold water. She ran her fingers through her hair and looked in the mirror.

"This is a nightmare," she whispered to her reflection. Oh, how she wished it were.

The next night Karin wrote in her journal . . .

*Last night is a blur. It was horrible. When Brian and Cindy came home, I couldn't stop crying. She wouldn't take anything for sleep because she said she wanted to be alert and strong for her children. She asked me to stay the night and I did. Kaitlin was asleep in her bed so I made a bed on the couch for Cindy. I sat in the recliner. Neither one of us slept. We talked quietly until the sun came up. Then she called her parents. They said they would take the first flight available. Then she called Don's parents. I heard his mother scream over the phone all those miles away.*

*Cindy seems like a rock; she has aged overnight. Her kids are her only concern at this point. When they woke this morning, they were pleased and sur-*

*prised to find Kaitlin there. We left then, and Cindy told them about their dad. Sarah is six, Stevie is four.*

*I saw Cindy's parents arrive this afternoon. I told her to call if they needed anything, but didn't wait for that. I made dinner and brought it over to them. They were pleased, as they hadn't given eating much thought. The kids don't really understand it yet, I'm sure. They are happy to have their grandparents there.*

*Don's parents arrived this evening. I can't imagine their pain. Their son was thirty-two years old. I can't write anymore.*

Brian called his office that morning and explained the situation. He would take the day off as he was up most of the night. He had been a great help to the grieving widow and her family. Karin had explained as best she could to Kaitlin.

"Don had been on his way home from bowling, and someone hit him on the driver's side, Honey." Kaitlin was terribly upset and wondered what she would do, if her dad died.

Cindy told Karin the night it happened, that she had waited up for him as she always did. He was usually home by eleven o'clock. She had fallen asleep on the couch and didn't wake until the phone rang at twelve-fifteen. Then she had run next door, and Karin knew the rest.

Brian and Karin sat in front of the fire and talked way into the next day many nights after that happened. It was just so unbelievable.

Karin didn't work at all that week; she couldn't. She took care of Cindy's kids when the family went to make funeral arrangements and did all the laundry, while she was there. Her heart ached every time she looked at those kids. Sarah asked her a few questions about "Daddy" and she had answered as best she could. She wished she could make things the way they were, but of course no one could.

The funeral was five days after the accident. It took that long for the families to gather. They all stayed at a motel, except Cindy's parents. They wanted to be near their daughter and help her anyway they could. Karin and Brian had met them once before, when they came for a visit. It had been a much happier time. They stayed for a week after everything was over and tried to talk Cindy into moving back home.

"I can't do anything yet, Karin, but my mother is so insistent. I don't know what to do," Cindy told her.

"She's just so worried about you, and she wants to take care of you, now. It's understandable, don't you think?"

"I know, but I don't want to do anything too quickly. I keep thinking, what would Don want me to do?" she said and started to cry. Karin took her hand.

"In time you may want to be close to your parents, Cindy. It would probably be good for the kids, too. Tell your mom you're thinking about that, but need time. I'm sure she'll understand. Your parents are so nice. I've gotten to know them a little better since they've been here this time."

"Oh, I know they are, and I don't know what I would have done without them now. I can't believe it yet, Karin. I will never see that man again. I can't quite get my mind around the thought of that." Karin couldn't either. Nor could she think of a thing to say, so she didn't say a word.

Weeks after Don was buried, Kaitlin told her mother that she didn't know what to say when she was with Cindy or the kids.

"Everyone feels like that after someone dies, Honey, but don't think you can't talk about it if they want to," she tried to explain.

"But I think if it's talked about, it will make them sad all over again."

"They will all be sad for a very long time, Kaitlin, but I've learned that people like to talk about a loved one who has died. They like to hear other people tell them things, too. Like the time Don took you and the kids to the park. Remember how much fun you had and how much you laughed that day?"

"Yeah, it was fun," she said, remembering it well.

"Things like that, but you can wait for them to bring up the subject. I'm sure they will, especially those kids. I'll bet Stevie won't even remember his dad when he grows up. It's so sad."

"He won't?" Kaitlin asked. She hadn't thought of that.

"Well, he's only four. Do you remember much about when you were that young?"

She thought a minute and shook her head. "I don't think I do," Kaitlin said, quietly. That night she wrote in her journal.

*Mom said today that Stevie maybe won't remember his dad who died. I worry about stuff like that sometimes. I don't know what I would do if one of my parents died. I don't even want Betsy to die, ever.*

# ~17~

It was a rough winter, not the weather necessarily, but the grieving was very difficult for Cindy and the kids, and so hard for their neighbors to watch.

"I think Cindy is doing so well, and then she will lose it again," Karin told Brian.

"I think that's how it goes. It's normal, I'm sure," he said. "She is doing well. She's taking care of her kids and everything else. If she stayed in bed all day, I would worry about her. She will grieve for a long time."

"I just wish I could do something. I feel so sorry for her."

"You are doing something. You're always here for her, and you help her with the kids. You even talk endlessly with her about Don. What you want to do is make it the way it was, but you can't. No one can," he said, softly.

"I suppose you're right," she said, quietly. "I want him to be there again. We had so much fun over the holidays, didn't we? I'll always remember that."

"I will, too. It was fun. I'll miss him this sum-

157

mer, when we work in the yard again. He and I always found time to talk then. Ah, it's just so sad," he said, pulling his wife close to him. He was so happy to share his life with her. She had changed some since her grandmother died, and he thought it was for the best. She was deeper, if that was the right word, and he truly cherished her. The change in her had come before the neighbor's death. It often takes something like that to awaken people to the importance of life, but not her.

*This morning, on my way to work, I saw a crocus poking through the snow that is still on the ground. It's like a promise every year, that spring will come again; the renewal of life. I love it.*

*Cindy is thinking of putting her house on the market and moving to be near her parents. I think it's an excellent idea, but I will miss her so much. We have become very close since Don's death. I told her I would help her with the selling of the house in any way I can. She decided to list it with Carson Realty.*

*Kaitlin wants to have a slumber party for her thirteenth birthday. Thirteen! Can it be possible? I think it will be fun. We will plan it together.*

She closed her journal and turned out the light. She carefully turned on her side so she wouldn't wake Brian, but then he reached for her.

"I thought you were asleep," she said, surprised.

"I was faking it. I was waiting for you," he whispered in her ear and pulled her closer to him.

~~~

*I asked Mom if I could have a slumber party for*

*my thirteenth birthday. A teenager at last! I want
to have Sharon, of course and maybe Barbara,
Carol, Mary Ann and Leslie. Six would be a good
number, I think, and they are my best friends. Well,
Sharon is my best; everyone knows that. Mom said
she would think about it. She's pretty sure we can
have it.*

*Yesterday I started my period. Mom was cool
about it. Sharon hasn't yet, but I'm sure she will
soon. I hope so anyway.*

*Betsy is getting big. She is in my bed now. I love
to sleep with her, but sometimes she is a* <u>*bed-hog*</u>*!*

~~~

"I can't tell you how much I'll miss you when we
move, Karin. I honestly don't know what I would
have done without you these past few months,"
Cindy said. The two women were having coffee in
Cindy's kitchen. Sarah and Kaitlin were at their
respective schools, and Stevie was napping in his
room. They did this often lately. It was good for
them both. Karin was happy to be home more, and
able to help this young widow with all she was going
through.

She felt good about being able to help, but wished
she didn't have to. That would mean the tragedy
had never happened and that the family was intact.
She wasn't one of those people who found joy in
rescuing people in trouble, but if someone needed
her, she was there.

~~~

*We listed Cindy's house today. I hope we get the
asking price as it is in such good shape. Don took
care of his house, the way he cared for his family.*

*I'm so saddened to think strangers will be living there soon, but know it is best for all three of them. We are very close now, but we still aren't family. It will be good for Stevie to be close to his grandpa. He will be a good role model, I know. I will miss Cindy so much. We have become best friends, even though I am a decade older. More, she isn't thirty yet. I think she will be this year. We have promised to write often and call, but it's not the same as running back and forth between our houses. It will be a loss for me, for sure, and Kaitlin, too. She has learned to love those kids a lot.*

~~~

Sunday, during the open house at Cindy's, she and the kids spent the afternoon at Karin and Brian's house. Stevie and Brian wrestled on the floor together. The little boy missed doing that with his dad. Then he took a nap and the girls went to the mall, leaving the men at home.

The open house was a success. Corrine told Cindy and Karin all about it, when it was over. Lots of people had gone through the house and two couples wanted to see it again after they talked it over some more.

"Is anytime okay with you, Cindy?" Corrine asked. "We would call first, of course."

"Yes, anytime is fine. I'm home most of the time," Cindy told her.

The following Sunday the house was again open. This time Karin showed it. The couple most interested, the people who had gone back during the week, came this time with a bid. Karin went to the office, when the open house was over, typed it up and presented it to Cindy.

"Looks good. I'll think about it and let you know in the morning, if that's okay, Karin," she said.

"That's fine, Cindy. I'll be in the office by nine o'clock. Or you can call me at home; either way is fine," she said, sounding a little sad. It really was happening so fast.

*I think Cindy's house is sold, sad to say. Oh, I know that's selfish of me. I'm happy for her as it's a good bid. It's what we wanted, a little under the asking price, but we priced it that way. It's fair for both parties, buyer and seller.*

*Her parents said they would come back and help her get ready for the move when it's time. We offered to help, too. Her parents are so eager for her to be close to them, that I think they would move her themselves. I hope they give her space, when she gets there.*

*She told me that her parents are looking for a house for her and the kids. She has told them what she wants. They have found a few for her to consider. She and the kids will live with her parents for a while, if they haven't found what she wants. She hopes that won't happen, but I also hope she doesn't take the first house to avoid that and told her so. She assured me she wouldn't. I wish I could help her at that end, too, but I can't. She wants a location and house where she can stay, so schools are a factor. I'm off work tomorrow. I'm glad. I have lots to do here. The slumber party is this weekend.*

That night, Kaitlin wrote,

*Only four more days until my slumber party. I can't wait. Sharon is coming over early to help. She wanted to, so I said, yes. Next time we go to the lake, Mom says she can come with us.*

*I like writing a journal. Last night I read the whole thing from the beginning. It was fun because I could never remember all the stuff that has happened. I think I might let Sharon read it, but no one else.*

The slumber party was indeed a success. The girls finally settled down at three o'clock in the morning, after eating everything in sight. They had barbecues and chips for supper, then sundaes a bit later. After a while they had birthday cake, and then pizza at midnight, and, of course, lots of cola.

"Aren't you afraid they'll puke on the carpet?" Brian asked, when he saw all the food.

"Oh, I *hate* that word," Karin said, laughing. "No, I don't think they will. This is what is done at a girl's slumber party, Dear. Guys don't understand."

*My party was so fun. We stayed up late and played all sorts of games and ate all night. The food was good. Everybody said so. They said it was the best party ever. I told Sharon about my journal and when everyone else was sleeping, I let her read it. She is sworn to secrecy and she wants to start one, too. Wouldn't that be something if we both did, and read each other's when we're old ladies!!!!!!! Her mother said she could go with us to the lake. I'm so glad. Good-night.*

# ~18~

On Karin's next day off she decided to bake her grandma's sweet rye bread. She brought the recipe home from the lake. She had never before attempted to make a yeast bread. Kneading the dough, was the tricky part, but as she kept doing it she could feel when it was right, as it was no longer sticky. She greased the large crockery bowl and put the dough in it, turning it over once to grease it on all sides. She covered it with a dish towel and set it on the stove to rise. It *looked* just like Grandma's. She hoped it would taste as good as hers. She felt rather proud of herself.

When Brian came home that evening from work he stopped in the doorway and breathed deeply. Something smelled wonderful, and he wondered what she had done today. He went into the kitchen and saw the freshly baked loaves on the counter. One was a little misshapen, but they looked pretty good for a first attempt.

They sliced the oddly shaped one for dinner and froze the rest. It was delicious.

"Mom, I didn't know you could make this bread.

Isn't this the kind that Grandma Beth used to make?" Kaitlin asked.

"Yes, it is. Does it taste as good as hers, though? I've never made it before."

"It's good," Kaitlin said, smearing butter on yet another piece.

"It is good, Karin. I think I'll bring my lunch to work tomorrow. This would make a great ham sandwich," Brian said. And so one whole loaf had disappeared.

*I'm so glad I thought to bring home Grandma's recipe for bread. I made it today and it turned out pretty well. It tasted great, but I must work on forming the loaves. I have three left in the freezer. I think I'll give one to Cindy. It's rather therapeutic for me, the kneading, I mean.*

~~~

*We don't have school next week on Friday because of Teacher's Institute. Mom says we can leave for the lake Thursday after school. Sharon has never been up there before. It will be great. I can't wait!*

~~~

*Next weekend we will go to the lake, and Sharon is going with us. We'll leave Thursday afternoon as there is no school the next day. It should be nice. I'm looking forward to the break. I can't believe I even entertained the idea of selling that place for a minute. Where was my mind?*

*Cindy will be moving in three weeks. I brought her a loaf of my bread. They all liked it, even Stevie, who is a picky eater. I'll miss them.*

~~~

*Sharon got a journal. It's a spiral notebook like mine, but hers is blue. We brought them with us to the lake. We are sitting on our bed, writing. She is just starting hers. We got here last night and had pizza for supper. Sharon likes it here. I'm so glad.*

*Today is cloudy and cold. We played monopoly and canasta all morning on our bed. Mom said we can go into town this afternoon. I told Sharon that if she comes here next winter, we can bring our ice skates and skate on the lake. It's thawing now so we can't. She let me read her journal. She writes good.*

*Tomorrow is Sunday already and we have to go home. I wish we could stay longer, so does Sharon. In the summer we can stay longer, Mom said.*

*We are riding in the car now and writing in our journals. Betsy is asleep between us. Dad says we can stop for lunch in the next town. I'm glad, we're hungry.*

~~~

*It's good to be back home. We had a nice time with the girls. They slept in the bed where Mom and I did all those years ago. It was a bit colder there than here as spring is always a little behind that far north. Brian and I walked over to visit Pete. He's doing pretty well, but he had a slight stroke, he said. His speech is slurred a little, but otherwise you wouldn't be able to tell. He plans to sell the place and move closer to his son.*

*The cat rode in the back seat with the girls. We didn't need the carrier. She doesn't mind riding in the car and sleeps most of the way.*

*I helped Cindy today, as I didn't work. We packed up almost all of their clothes and all of her china. The house looks very different. The moving van will be there in a few days. Her parents are flying here tomorrow. They will drive her car back home, stopping along the way to make it a bit of a vacation. Cindy and the kids will fly to their new home in one week.*

*They should be settled in a few weeks time. They will stay with her parents until then. I hope it works out. There are two houses for her to choose from. They have narrowed it down to that with pictures and many phone calls. Her parents have helped her so much. I miss her already.*

~~~

*There is the cutest boy in school!!! He just moved here and he's in our math class. Sharon likes him, too. He doesn't talk very much because he doesn't know anyone, I guess. I wish he would!!*

~~~

*I watched as the moving van backed up to Cindy's this morning. I had such an odd sensation in my stomach. It's really happening. The people who bought the house seem very nice, but it won't be the same.*

*I'm really busy at work, now. I have lots to do. Spring is always like this - it's good.*

*We took Cindy out for a nice dinner at a fancy restaurant tonight. Sort of a farewell dinner, I guess. Kaitlin stayed with the kids; it will be the last time. We had a nice dinner and talked awhile after. She's doing well, I think. I don't know how she does it. We talked a great deal about Don and how much their friendship meant to us. We cried a little and decided to have a sweet dessert.*

~~~

*I babysat for Sarah and Stevie tonight. Mom and Dad took Cindy out for dinner. It's the last time I'll take care of them. I will miss them. They are nice kids. Not brats, like some.*

~~~

*Kaitlin is growing up so fast, and she is turning into a beautiful young woman. She is sweet and seems very sensible. What more could a mother ask? Sharon is much like her and they are best friends still, even with all the changes they are going through. They seem good for each other. I pray they stay as they are. They are good kids. I see so many girls with tattoos, pierced eyebrows and tongues, with maroon colored hair and I say a silent prayer of thanks. We have spent much time discussing what is expected of her as she grows up. So far, so good!*

*Received a letter from Cindy today with pictures of their new home. It's beautiful! She included a short note to Kaitlin from Sarah. She prints very well; it was sweet. They seem to be doing okay. I'm so glad.*

~~~

*Sarah wrote to me and sent a picture of their house. It's really pretty. I still miss them.*

~~~

*I am alone in the house for the night. Well, Betsy is here with me. Brian is out of town on business and Kaitlin is spending the night with Sharon. I welcome the respite, only because I know it is for one night. It's damp and chilly tonight, so I lit the fireplace. We are well into spring, but tonight the fire feels good.*

*Karol called today to tell me that their oldest son has become engaged. She says the girl is a bit of a space queen, but nice. Karol's mouth will never change. I wonder when the wedding will be. It's a chance for us to go for a visit. She said they are all fine.*

*I had a microwave dinner tonight and ate in front of the television. A definite no-no in this house. Betsy and I watched <u>On Golden Pond</u>. I love that movie. Brian bought it for me years ago, and every once in a while I watch it again.*

*We are now in bed together. She is curled against my legs. I can't believe how much company this little creature is. She's very comforting somehow, and I'm glad we decided to take her.*

*Brian called a bit ago. Everything went well at the seminar and he will be back in town tomorrow around noon.*

*I am surprised to see how quickly this book is filling up with my writing. One of these days I'll read through it . . .*

She had fallen asleep, sitting straight up in bed with her journal in her lap, just as she had done all those months ago at the lake house; a changed woman, however. She was content with her life now, more than she had ever been, and she had learned that lesson from her grandmother's writing. She would continue to keep a journal as long as she could, with the hope that her daughter would learn from and enjoy her writing as much as she had her beloved grandmother's.

She woke slightly and closed the book, then reached up and turned off the light. Turning on her side, she pulled up her legs. This aroused the cat, who stood up, stretched her entire length, circled and settled softly behind Karin's knees. They slept this way until the sun rose.

# About the Author

K. M. Swan started writing when she was in her fifties. After High School she trained to be a registered nurse, married, raised four children and practiced nursing part-time. She now has three grandchildren and enjoys writing about things that are important to her.

# The Novels of
# K. M. Swan

If you enjoyed reading *The Journals* and would like additional copies or information about her other novels:

- *The Loft*
- *Catherine's Choice*
- *Sarah*

Please mail your request to:

K. M. Swan
P.O. Box 8673
Rockford IL 61126

E-mail: kmswanbooks@aol.com

Or check your local bookstore for availability.